ARTIFACTS

MEMORIES OUT OF SPACE AND TIME

WILLIAM JONES

Copyrights

"A Change of Life," appeared in *Dark Wisdom*, Elder Signs Press, 2005.
— appeared in *Hardboiled Cthulhu*, Dimensions Books, 2006.

"Feasters of the Dark," appeared in #2, *Dreaming in R'leyh*, 2003.
— appeared in *Secrets of New York*, Chaosium, 2005.
— appeared in *Dark Covenants*, Naked Snake Press, 2005.

"Rawhide and Bloodybones," appeared in *Darkness Rising 2005*, Prime Books, 2005.

"Rusting Edge," appeared in *Vortex* (original format), 1996.

"The Name of the Enemy," appeared in *Horrors Beyond*, Elder Signs Press, 2005.

"The Tiger," appeared in *Dark Furies*, Die Monster Die Books, 2005.
— appeared in In *Lovecraft's Shadows*, Tenoka Press, 2006.

"Wind Demons," appeared in *Hell's Hangmen*, Tenoka Press, 2006

FIRST EDITION
10 9 8 7 6 5 4 3 2 1
Published in February 2007
ISBN:978-0-9779876-9-6
Printed in the U.S.A.

Published by Distant Light Books
P.O. Box 389
Lake Orion, MI 48361-0389

ARTIFACTS

MEMORIES OUT OF SPACE AND TIME

WILLIAM JONES

DISTANT
LIGHT

2007

"The Fancy is indeed no other than a mode of memory emancipated from the order of time and space."
—Samuel Taylor Coleridge

"Time moves in one direction, memory in another."
—William Gibson

CONTENTS

TALES OF A STRANGE FUTURE

TALES OF A CURIOUS PAST

TALES OF A
STRANGE FUTURE

THE TIGER

A NEVER-ENDING CADENCE OF rain tapped upon the roof. There seemed no limit to the deluge. From the moment Caley Faith Dayton had arrived in Hillston, there had been no indication of the storm relenting. Nonetheless, she remained in position, buried in the darkness, waiting.

Lights flashed in the driveway.

On schedule, Caley thought. From inside the empty house, she discerned the target's SUV. A muted thud filled the hallway as the front door slammed, the storm quickly consumed the sound.

No light filled the house as the target stumbled through the darkened hallway.

Odd. Then the image of Hillston in complete darkness flicked through her mind. When she'd been airlifted into the town that existed in the center of a dead volcanic caldera, there had been no lights. The entire town had been shrouded in a palpable blackness. At the time she'd fancied it a result of the storm. But now an elusive thought danced at the fringe of her mind, a melody she couldn't remember, there but always out of reach.

As the target approached, she raised the silenced Beretta.

As he neared, there came a faint hissing, a hand sliding against a wall, guiding him down the murky corridor. That sound mingled with the knocking rain, sending a tiny chill down the length of Caley's spine. *That* worried her.

The target ambled closer.

She'd been designed, engineered for this work. She didn't get chills or tingles — except at times when the geneticists had left the primal emotion as a warning. *Fear.* It had been keyed low so as not to stir panic; it served to caution her — nothing more. Another tool in her craft.

The target glided past the doorway, a dark figure stepping from the shadows and returning to them. Caley did not take the shot. The fear, ever so slight, had stayed her finger. And it continued to well inside her like rain filling a hole. The depth grew, and so did its meaning.

Now light flickered from the room beyond.

Caley recognized the glow of a computer. Probably a laptop on a battery, she decided. Tapping keys joined the tapping of the downpour.

Slowly, Caley slinked forward, testing the floor, feeling for the slightest give that might transform into a creak.

The target sat hunched before a laptop, typing, fiddling with something at the computer's side, and then typing again. Water puddled on the wooden floor beneath him. His hair and clothes clung to his wiry frame, heavy and sodden.

Although she could see the screen over the man's shoulder, it made little sense.

A sudden flash of light filled the room, followed by the deep snarl of thunder. From the corner of her eye, Caley glimpsed a silhouette framed in the window. But before she could focus on it, the figure dashed away.

Gooseflesh spilled over her, awakening a deeper fear buried inside her mind — primitive and feral.

Ignorant to the unfolding drama beyond the microcosm of his world, the man continued to jab at keys with an increasingly frenzied pace.

Something was wrong, and Caley needed to know what it was before she went any further. Too many alarms had been triggered in her mind. The situation had changed drastically from her original briefing. This wasn't a straightforward as-sassination.

"Hey!" she called out. "Time to give the computer a rest."

The man spun, nearly falling from the chair, then hurriedly scrambling to his feet. His eyes cast about, attempting to focus upon Caley. The display backlit him, creating a blue aura around his form. It would take a few moments for his eyes to adjust.

"Who are you?" he asked, his voice cracking. "What are you doing in here?"

"I've got the gun —" she jabbed it against his chest — "so I ask the questions."

His head shifted back and forth as he tried to locate her in the darkness.

"First," Caley started, "what are *you* doing?"

He hesitated a moment — too long for him to speak the truth. "I'm just transferring files." His hands lifted.

"No-no," Caley warned. "Keep the hands at your sides. Speak with your mouth."

"I . . . I was just going to clean the water from my glasses," he stammered.

"Not now. You're answering questions. So let's start over. If you lie again, I'm just going to fuckin' shoot you and be on my way." *Which I should have done already*, she chided herself.

Seconds passed as he absorbed the concept, but it didn't take as long as others Caley had killed.

"If you want money, I have some in my wallet and a little more upstairs–"

"Don't piss me off," Caley interrupted. "One more chance."

He licked his lips as though preparing the way for the answer. "I was transferring files. I work for Patel Global — here in Hillston."

The tone and the quiver in his voice indicated he was telling the truth, but nothing Caley didn't already know. "You're telling me there's a deep black facility here?" She played coy. If there wasn't, then *she* wouldn't be here.

For a few heartbeats the man stood transfixed. "I didn't say anything about deep black."

Caley shook her head. "Are you fuckin' brain dead? You must be a mathematician. They can never add up a real life situation to save their lives." A slick giggle escaped her when she realized her joke. "I'm here to kill you. Sent by your employer. That either means you scored low on your last performance review, or you are a security breach in a black-ops program. Now which do want to go with?"

It was as if the man's visage had deflated. His lids drooped, his mouth slumped at the corners, even his body seemed to sag. "I work at the Temple," he said with a voice nearly washed away by the rain.

"What's the project?" Her protocols prohibited her from asking such questions, or any questions for that matter. Her function was to simply eliminate problems. However, the feeling hounding her made it easy to overlook the rules.

"We were attempting to alter spatial barriers, and influence higher dimensions," he said with a slight haughty flavor. "Instead we opened a doorway to some place in Earth's past." He shrugged, then made a noise that only slightly resembled a laugh.

Another quick flash of lightning and the quake of thunder filled the caldera. Heavy weather was moving in, and Caley didn't want to be here any longer than she needed. If the storm got much thicker, she'd lose her ride.

"Let's try another approach," Caley said, lifting the gun to prevent the egghead from cooking up a stupid idea. "What's with the lights in this town?"

"I don't know. We had a malfunction at the Temple. I tried to stay. When I came out, everything was dark." His jaw clenched. "I stayed until nearly everyone was killed. The facility was locked down, but I bypassed the security."

"So you *are* a mathematician," Caley said.

"No, a physicist. I took the project leader's passcard."

She shook her head. If these eggheads *ever* paid attention to the rumors, they'd figure out that everyone who pulls this trick ends up missing. She found it difficult to believe that someone like this guy had played with her genetics to produce her. Then she decided that someone like her, if not her, probably killed him shortly thereafter.

A crash echoed through the house, glass shattering, followed by a heavy thud. Nightmarish thoughts raced through her mind like a flame that had just ignited an explosion. Her heart slammed against her ribs.

Caley eyed the scientist as she listened to the thick scampering of what sounded to be an impossibly large insect — one with far too many legs.

She leveled the Beretta at his chest. In the blue radiance of the laptop, her keen vision spied his angular visage, dark eyes deepened by the lack of sleep, the nervous tautness of his features, and a desperate struggle to control a faint shudder.

"What's your name?" she asked, releasing the tension from the pistol's trigger. Her mind — her programming — told her to finish the task. But a deeper, far older instinct urged her to keep the target alive.

"Graham Douglass," he muttered.

"I need to know what goes on at the Temple," she said flatly. "If you lie, I will kill you. Understand? From this point on, there is no detail you keep from me. Don't try any of that *classified* bullshit, either." She wagged the Beretta. "I've got clearance."

Graham nodded.

The rapid fire drumming of something moving sounded from the second floor.

"The work there is compartmentalized," he started. "We are not shown the big picture. That way–"

With a fluid motion, Caley elevated the pistol to the center of Graham's forehead. Gently, like the blessed kiss of a priest, she pressed it against his damp flesh.

"But . . . I . . . I do know some of what the other teams are up to. After a while, you can figure it out." The words poured forth like a long held confession. "We always do. I mean, no one talks about it. But the requests and the lab construction and topics we are told to avoid eventually fit together and form an outline of what's missing. If you think about it, you can figure it out . . . sometimes."

"*Point*, Graham. I'm looking for a point." Caley pulled the pistol from his head, not to put him at ease, but because the noise upstairs had stopped, leaving only his voice and the ceaseless driving rain to fill the room.

"My job was to construct a device that produced specific quantum wave field collapses. The specs required sustained–"

Caley turned her cold eyes upon him. "I'm put off by technobabble," she said icily. "Translate."

Graham nodded, closed his eyes and narrowed his lips as though searching for the right words.

"Superstring theory–"

Annoyed, Caley made a show of checking the Beretta. "Don't start with that shit. Translate, or you're useless to me."

"All right . . . My job is to make a hole in the fabric of the universe," he said, frustrated. "A tunnel that stretched from our time in space to another. I think the objective of the project was to peer into the past, like an inter-dimensional telescope, except with enough energy — a vast amount of energy — a tunnel could be maintained, allowing for matter to be transferred as well."

A hurried and violent scampering trailed across the ceiling, as something commenced moving again. Graham hushed as the noise grew louder.

With a soft and stealthy movement, Caley sidled to the doorway, Beretta held in both hands, angled down.

From around the corner came a sickly, watery gurgling. Sharp needles hopped along her arms. Dread gripped her. This wasn't a precaution left in her genetics as a warning; it was an oversight, DNA that her creators didn't understand.

A faint creak sounded. A creature cautiously emerged, slouching into view. For a moment it stood motionless, impossibly still, in a timeless custom performed between predator and prey.

Caley tried to make sense of what stood before her. The size of a dog, it possessed at least six hinged legs that, although appearing clumsy, worked with a graceful liquid motion. Black stubby hair glistened from the rain or the monstrosity's own secretions — from the rancid odor, Caley guessed the latter. Knotty masses of flesh resembling tumors dotted its form, protruding from the slick coat, giving it the appearance of something in transformation. A black maw lined with pearly teeth, vertically split its massive head. Eyes winked and shone in the wan light, countless, all gazing in different directions. The abomination nauseated Caley and terrified her, forming a cold mass in her stomach.

A sonorous growl issued from the creature.

"*Fuck you.*"

Three shots snipped from the silenced Beretta. She dashed to the other side of the doorway, firing three more. The creature quivered as the 9mm slugs entered its body. A split-second later it collapsed.

Caley stepped forward and fired a solitary shot directly into its head. In the faint muzzle flash, she spied its several eyes transfixed on some distant point. The slug sliced through the skull, smacking the floor beneath it. Blood oozed forth.

Graham now stood in the corner of the room, his eyes like the creature's, wide and locked in a dead gaze.

Caley pulled the clip from the pistol and slapped in another. "This come from the Temple?"

"Yes," Graham replied, pulling his eyes from the dead thing. "That's not what we found. That's the result. What we found was more basic. Primordial. It was the source of life on this world. Even though it was amorphous, it was aware — you could *feel* it. Once we had opened the tunnel, it probed our minds. It took control of some people, beckoning them to join it."

"You mean be eaten?"

"Consumed, yes. But not eaten. Joined. Its thoughts . . . desires filled my mind. Cajoling me, yearning for me to share its consciousness. Those who entered the tunnel melted into it."

"We're back to eaten," she added, then continued for him. "And you alerted someone. And they told you to stay put and secure the Temple."

Graham nodded, quick jerky motions. "You stayed for a while, but finally you left. They knew you would. So I was pulled into this fuckin' mess because some goddamn egghead can't die like he's fuckin' supposed to? Is that the story?"

"No," Graham said, stepping forward. "What we were doing was science. What happened was an accident."

"Oh, I know this part. Here's where you tell me that science is humanity's great hope. That without it we are doomed to ignorance. And never once do you eggheads ever stop to see that science has become your own private god. The facility is even called 'The Temple.'"

Burning with rage, she marched to the window. Rain flowed over the glass as thick as oil. The world beyond was distorted and dark, not even the heavens cut through the storm. As she surveyed the gloomy vista before her, a verse of a long forgotten poem came unbidden:

When the stars threw down their spears,
And watered heaven with their tears,
Did he smile his work to see?
Did he who made the lamb make thee?

After a few moments, Caley said, "How many are out there?"

"I don't know. I cut the Temp . . . the facility's power. The tunnel closed, but some had already escaped. Once the amorphous creature had joined with a human, it started releasing progeny. Inhuman creations. Crawling arms and slithering spinal cords, all with legs from insects or animals. Monsters. Once they were loose . . ."

"They consumed every living thing they encountered — calling them to *join* it," Caley finished, pointing to the dead creature. "I can feel it in my head right now. It's calling me."

"Ignore it," Graham pleaded. "You have to."

Caley continued to watch the dark world beyond the slick window. Thunder rumbled in the distance each time that lightning illuminated the horizon.

"Don't listen to it," Graham tried again.

"Shut up. Both you and it are really giving me a headache." She turned to face the scientist whom she'd been sent to kill. She too was the handiwork of his god, and that pissed her off. And somewhere along the way, she'd become the savior for when science screwed up.

Realization flashed across his countenance. In the bluish glow, Caley saw lines of tension running along the edge of his eyes and mouth.

"I'm not going to kill you," she said dully. "I'm guessing your new pets will do that."

His eyes remained fixed upon her for a long moment, then he cast about, like a man waking from a nightmare, not sure of where he was. "We need to let the world know," he said, returning to the computer. "I bet that Patel Global shut down the town's power. They know what's loose here. Somehow, I think they knew what we would find all along. Our directives were too precise, too narrow in scope for them not to have known."

"You're a fast learner," Caley said, then strolled out of the room.

"What are you doing?" Graham asked, frustration and terror shaping his words.

The eggheads had always been expendable. She'd had her own epiphany. This little town in a volcanic caldera was an experiment. Containable and distant enough to terminate if things went wrong. A petri dish. But Patel Global, those running the show, would burn the entire town if they needed.

"I'm leaving," Caley said, returning to the room where she'd been hiding.

"We can't let this happen," Graham said. "This is wrong. If these creatures leave this town they could infect the world."

She hefted her duffle bag and settled it over a shoulder. "It's not my fuckin' world. It never was."

Again came the sensation of something shifting inside her head, as though a worm were squirming through her brain, touching upon memories. Then she felt the calling again. There were no words, only a feeling of belonging. A faint desire to be embraced.

Graham dropped to his knees, hands clamped against his head in a vise-like hold. "No!" he cried. "I won't!"

Perhaps, Caley decided, she had a slight immunity to the telepathic probing. Score one for the eggheads who drew-up her blueprints.

She watched as Graham sprawled on the floor, wiggling as though trying to hide from the pain inside his head. For Caley it was distant and fuzzy.

Finally, she grabbed Graham by the arms, hoisting him upward, slamming him against the wall. "If you keep acting like that, I am going to kill you," she said angrily. "Push it out of your mind. You can muster enough willpower to do that, can't you?"

He flinched and danced in her grip, eyes rolled up as though he were looking to Heaven for help. Slobbery gasps escaped his mouth as he choked and gagged, and then he slumped and fell silent.

Caley shook him. "Wake up. We're leaving," she said. "And you're driving."

* * *

The SUV sluiced down Green Street, heading southwest toward the city's heart. The brewing storm continued to roil. Lightning flashed, revealing the encircling mountains that were bearded with thick conifers and carved with steep slopes.

Slanted sheets of water crashed into the windshield with the fat *thump* of bullets. Through the downpour, Caley gazed at the hollow-faced Victorian style houses edging the street, the last remnants of a once thriving mining town. Black and empty windows returned her gaze.

"Which direction is the Temple?" she asked.

"Northeast of here — behind us."

"Is this the only way out of the town?" she asked.

"There are train cuts in the mountains, but we'd have to walk."

"No good. I don't intend to be ambushed in a culvert. And those will be blocked soon enough — if not already."

Anger continued to smolder in her gut as she thought about this half-assed plan. One egghead tipped the entire bucket of shit, when all she had to do was pull the trigger after he entered the house. If she'd just done that, the mess would be behind her, and she'd be out of here. She needed him now, in case she didn't have a way out. He knew things. To the people who pulled the strings, the egghead was her bargaining chip. She just needed to convince them.

"You're wrong, you know," Graham said, unexpectedly.

As the vehicle hit the Cement Creek Bridge, the tires hummed across the surface. Over the rail, the creek swelled, threatening to pour into the town. Although she didn't know how, Caley sensed a connection between the storm and the creatures, and the solitary *mind* they possessed.

"About what?" she asked.

"It is your world. It didn't leave you. You left it."

She laughed harshly. "You're wrong there. I was never part of it. It never cared for me. This —" she pointed at the view before her — "this is so fucked up that I don't want to be a part of it."

As they approached downtown Hillston, Caley caught quick flickers of movement — shadows stealing through the dark, vague shapes lurking around the corners of the houses.

"Put some speed on," she said.

The SUV accelerated.

"Why do you do it, if you don't like it?" Graham asked.

"Where did you get that idea?" she said fiercely. "You think because I didn't kill you, I don't like what I do? You think because I'm stuck in another fucked-up experiment that I'm rethinking who I am?" Her anger kindled as she spoke, each word building the flame. "Are you a physicist or a fuckin' psychiatrist?"

"I didn't think any of those things. Interesting that *you* mentioned them, however."

"Shut up and drive."

The streets counted down as they approached the edge of town: 10th, 9th, 8th Street. Then Caley spotted a flash to the vehicle's left. A bright burst of light, followed by a muffled *thump*.

"Stop," she said.

"Why? We're almost out of town."

"Stop!" she ordered, pulling the Beretta from its holster underneath her jacket. "I think it might be too late to leave."

Graham slowed the vehicle to a stop, pulling along the curb. "What do you mean?"

"I saw something over there." She pointed.

"Probably lightning."

"No. It was a grenade. Unless the local sheriff has an impressive arsenal, I'm guessing the military has already cordoned the town."

She opened the door. "I'm going to check it out. If you see anyone but me return, pull off fast. Head anywhere but where you were going. I'll find you."

Deftly, she jumped from the vehicle. When she turned to shut the door, she was surprised to see an unspoken concern shaping his countenance. "I'm not doing this for you, so don't fool yourself." Rain pelted her jacket, black as the night.

"I understand," he said. "Should I turn off the headlights?"

"Nope. They already know we're here. Just wait as long as you can."

With that, Caley slipped into the rain and the darkness.

When she came upon the site, there was no doubt a grenade had been used. Shattered windows, gutted earth, and two dead creatures told the tale. She crept from one location to the next, taking cover and listening as she went. No need to risk examining the corpses, even though they were not like the one she'd killed. Both were larger. She estimated at least waist high when they stood on all fours, or sixes — she wasn't sure. The one that remained mostly intact had leathery rolls of skin that formed thick bands of flesh around its tubular body, and it sported claws as deadly as any combat knife. Its head seemed to be recessed into its mass, protected by a thick hide. And it still possessed the hideous teeth and a vertical mouth. But now the eyes were all pointing forward, like those of a predator.

Are they evolving? she wondered. *Can they change that quickly?* In the back of her mind she heard a disturbing answer. Again, she felt the calling.

A noise came from above her. She stood beneath the awning of a house, back to the wall.

They can feel my mind, she told herself. *No stealth when they can do that.*

With practiced motion, she edged sideways, holding the pistol upward, waiting for the thing to pounce.

After a few paces, it lunged down, landing on the ground, standing. This one had eight legs and a bulbous torso, much like an gigantic spider. Water washed along its coarse hide, its eyes, myriad eyes, were soulless, black and brimming with cruelty. As it stirred, its legs shifted up and down, effortlessly conveying its tremendous bulk. It was much, much larger than the others.

There was no outrunning it. And she desperately wanted to do just that, because it filled her with a feeling alien to her: A primitive and ferocious terror that sliced through her mind.

She braced herself against the wall, slowly raising the pistol.

The calling filled her mind again, this time stronger, more alluring. She imagined it to be like the beckon of a beloved parent — something that was also alien to her.

Shapes moved behind the grotesque creature. One by one they snapped around the distant corner of a neighboring house, proficient and economic.

Just as the creature hulked toward her, Caley dropped low, landing on the muddy ground, firing as she went.

A hail of shots streamed from behind the monstrosity. Automatic weapons, firing bursts. Like the rain, the shots came in torrents. Flesh tore from the creature's body, thick blood splashed into the night's shroud. Rounds slammed into the wall where Caley had been standing, burrowing into the clapboard house. Within a second, the creature lay dead, legs twitching, jaws snapping as life drained away.

"Dayton?" came a gravelly voice.

"Caley," she replied, knowing the procedure.

"Caley Dayton?"

"Caley Faith Dayton," she answered. "If you're done with the bullshit, I'd like to get up."

"Following orders," said a solider garbed in black. He tromped through the mud, boots splashing as he approached. Behind him four others formed, each at the ready, scouring the night in different directions.

"Lieutenant Warner," the man said, slinging his assault rifle. "I'm here to extract you."

He stood an inch or two taller than she. He had a worn, rugged demeanor about him, but his mask and uniform hid all other features, except his eyes. In that brief moment, she had sized him up, and decided she could handle him without much problem.

"I have a civilian with me."

The eyes remained upon her. They held no warmth, only a bleak emptiness. Nothing existed in them except the consideration for duty. "My orders regard only you."

Caley pushed past the lieutenant, knocking him aside. "You're telling me that the civilian's life doesn't score here?" She entered into the circle of soldiers. They ignored her, continuing to search the night for hostiles.

Warner trailed behind. "The civilian is not my concern."

"Halt!" one of the soldiers cried.

Without turning, Caley cocked her head toward Warner and said, "It looks like he is now." *The stupid fuck! I told him to stay with the vehicle.*

"I'm halted," Graham called out.

"Drop your weapon," a soldier ordered.

Something hit the soggy ground. "It's only a lug wrench. Not much of a weapon given the scheme of things."

Although he faced Caley, Warner's lifeless eyes glanced beyond her at the scientist. They seemed dead. She'd seen those eyes many times in her life, mostly in the mirror. The thoughts lurking behind that callous stare were all too familiar.

"Warner, don't," she said softly.

His attention returned to her, but he gave no response.

"How long before the site is cleansed?" she asked, trying to hold his attention. Inside her heart pounded like it never had before. The ritual had always been cold and mechanical; she'd never felt these emotions in the past.

"One hour, at the most. We drop back in twenty, and set up a new perimeter. All exits are mined — sealed." He lifted his head to the surrounding mountains. "I think the slopes are too rugged for anything to get out, but we're scorching everything to be sure. That way–" he waved a hand at the surrounding houses — "the slate is wiped. Including any *oversights*."

"Take him," Caley said. "He knows things."

Warner ignored her, turning to speak to his team. Caley stepped back and kicked high. The resounding *crack* told her that Warner was dead before he had hit the ground.

"Drop, Graham!" she yelled, as the remaining soldiers spun to face her.

Swift with fury, Caley was in their midst, grabbing one by his flak jacket and hurling him into the next. Adrenaline surged through her body, adding strength, fueling wrath. The geneticists who brewed her had been good with what they did understand. And they had intended for her to be a killer.

Using the soldier in her grasp as an anchor, she kicked at the knee of the next. Effortlessly her booted foot snapped bone and ripped tendon. As another soldier attempted to push his way into the mass, she released her grip, letting her anchor fall backward, splashing to the muddy earth.

A combat blade slashed at her, its surface glistening as it sliced through the rain and night. She dropped low, fanning a leg at the man's ankles, easily tumbling him.

Quickly, she launched herself upward, pulling a blade from her boot as she did. Like a phantom, she carved with ruthless rage at the oncoming soldiers. Her actions were quick and light, precise and deadly. After a moment, she stood alone, amidst the dead bodies, combat blade in hand, with a slick red surface.

Graham clambered to his feet, slipping in the muck. "Why?" he asked, dismayed. "They were here to help us."

She wiped the blade on the grass, shaking her head. "You have too much faith," she answered. "They were here to tie up loose ends."

As she approached Graham, he made no movement, gave no indication of fleeing.

"This is an old mining town, right?" she asked.

"Yes. Most of the old mines are closed. One was used by the Temple, and another was being built up for expansion." He twisted his head, peeking into the blackness through his water-specked glasses. He looked like a nearsighted, nearly drowned mouse. "The houses used to be the homes of the workers." There was a lonesome quality in his voice. "Why?"

"That's one I can't answer," Caley said, checking her watch. "It's a fucked up world. But you need to get us to the expansion shaft. If it's built to spec, we should make it through the next few hours."

Graham rubbed his head. Caley too felt the calling. It seemed remote, and for the first time she sensed a tinge of panic in it. Effortlessly she pushed it from her mind. In its place returned more lines from the long forgotten poem:

> *Tyger! Tyger! burning bright*
> *In the forests of the night,*
> *What immortal hand or eye,*
> *Dare frame thy fearful symmetry?*

"Move it," she said, pushing Graham forward. "One way or the other, it will be gone tomorrow. Just keep ignoring it."

As they tromped toward the SUV, the rain slackened. Caley knew they were in the eye of the storm. It wouldn't last for long.

ARTIFACTS

CLARE RASKIND WATCHED THE indent through the comm-center window as she struggled with the transceiver. Rain hammered the roof above, an unrelenting *thumping* sound that gnawed at her nerves. The rain, mixed with sultry heat, made Ceres a humid, tropical hell.

For nearly every day of her three-month rotation on the nightmarish jungle world, it had rained with only brief respites between the downpours, as though the planet were taking a breath between the measures of an endless song of rain. It was only the archeological work that kept Clare on this godforsaken world. Even so, there were days when she longed for her climate-controlled life on Mars. This rotation had been worse than others. Now she was just biding her time, waiting for the supply ship to bring fresh personnel and return her home for a six-month reprieve. Maybe a permanent reprieve, she thought as she gazed through the window.

Frustrated by the indent's lack of progress, Clare pulled a poncho over her head and marched into the deluge.

The indent had been tugging and yanking on transceiver components for almost fifty minutes, and there was still no uplink to the orbiting sats. Mud sloshed beneath Clare's boots as she trudged across the compound.

Drawing close, she caught snatches of the indent's curses, though the rain's frenetic tapping on her poncho drowned out most of his words.

"What's the problem?" she yelled above the storm, hoping to

attract his attention. Clare didn't like touching indents. True, the implants restricted violent behavior, but she was still reticent. Even though the Ministry had certified all of the ones on-site as being "rehabilitated," she preferred to keep her distance whenever possible. In many ways, Clare found the indents more alien than the civilization she studied on Ceres.

This was especially true about Kyne. Of the three indents assigned to the facility, Kyne seemed the most distant. There was a brooding coldness about him.

Kyne looked up when she spoke. A yellow poncho hood framed his face; water beaded, streaming over his skin. He rose from a crouch, tossing the interface deck into the mud.

"What?" he asked angrily.

Clare repeated her question, slowly. "What is the problem?"

"I don't know what the fuckin' problem is," Kyne exploded. "*That's* the problem. I'm a *laborer*–" he said the word slowly, as though mocking her. "Not a tech."

Clare stepped closer, hoping the distance would remind Kyne of her authority. She had to remain in control of the situation.

She'd been an archeologist all of her life. Only with this expedition had she become the project coordinator, a sour duty that kept her away from the real work in the field.

"It has a self-diagnostic. Use that. Don't try to guess the problem yourself." Her words came in short bursts, vying with the rumbling thunder and driving rain.

A bitter laugh escaped Kyne in a series of staccato grunts. "This thing is broken," he said. "It's not gonna fix itself. And it's not gonna tell me how to fix it." The indent's thick voice had no difficulty carrying over the storm. "Every time I slap a component in, it tells me to try again. I've used every replacement we got, and it still tells me it can't 'locate orbital link.'"

"Well, I'm certain beating it up isn't helping," Clare replied.

A slick smile pushed across Kyne's face. "I can't beat it up, remember?" He turned, trudging to the dormitory. "Give it a shot," he called over his shoulder. "Maybe you can *order* it to work."

Before Clare could respond, she was interrupted by the distant whine of an approaching shuttle.

* * *

The exhaust vents of the LH-T14 shuttle blasted sheets of water off the tarmac, mixing the already warm liquid with super-heated air. The pitch of the engines lowered abruptly as the squat transport dropped to a landing with a heavy *thump.*

Clare hurried toward it. The camp's other five members had been scheduled for a ten-hour field trip, working sites and observing Ceres' natives. Clare wondered what had brought them back six hours early.

A door on the side of the shuttle opened, half lifting upward, half lowering, forming a ramp. Before Clare could enter, Ita and David burst forth, carrying a stretcher between them.

"We have to get him to the infirmary," Ita yelled frantically.

Rain and blood streaked across her face. Deep, ruby stains spotted the front of her overalls. David trotted behind, sharing the burden of the stretcher. Dark gashes crossed his visage. Lying unconscious on the stretcher was Kesin. Raw, gaping slashes puckered on his chest, revealing black pools of blood.

"What happened?" Clare asked, keeping pace.

They rushed through the open hangar, down the narrow corridors to the infirmary.

Ita and David lowered Kesin onto the examination table while Clare activated the medical Aspect — a cyber-intellect that acted as the expedition's physician.

Within moments, a transparent shell lowered over the examination table, sealing Kesin inside. Probes tipped with sensors pierced his flesh, examining and inspecting his wounds.

The Aspect worked quickly to stabilize its human patient, suturing wounds and administering medication.

"Are you two all right?" Clare asked as the Aspect attended to Kesin.

Ita had backed against a wall, and slumped to the floor, arms hugging her knees. She sobbed, eyes closed, occasionally gasping for breath.

David, on the other hand, stared blankly, resting on a neighboring examination table.

"David, what happened?"

"We tried to contact you," he said. His words were as distant as his stare. "We couldn't get through."

"The transceiver is down," Clare said. "We've been working on it." She looked to Ita, then back to David. "Tell me what happened."

"We were exploring the ruins when we found the remains of a creature —" he shook his head — "or so we thought. It was just outside one of the destroyed cities, bordering the jungle. Kesin started recording it. And it came to life — started moving. He tried to get closer. Then . . ." David's voice faded, lost in the tapping of the rain.

Clare looked to Ita, but she was still huddled on the floor, sobbing.

After a moment, David's gaze returned to Clare from the distant place he had been watching.

"It was alive — some kind of animal," he muttered, his words softly rippling through the sterile infirmary air.

"It wasn't an animal!" Ita said frantically. "It was more like a machine, but alive inside."

Sensing the growing panic in Ita, Clare retrieved a sedative from the dispensary.

"You need to rest," Clare said, approaching Ita.

"It doesn't feel anything!" Ita cried, burying in her head in her hands. "It wants to kill us. I could feel the hatred in its mind."

"Don't think about it," Clare said, injecting Ita with the sedative. "You're safe now."

"No! We're not safe! We got to get off this world." Her words slurred as the drug swaddled her mind in a blanket of sleep. "It can feel our presence . . . ."

Ita was the only expedition member who had been genetically enhanced to be a sensitive — Talent was what the *genginers* called it. She didn't have the ability of a telepath, but she sometimes felt the emotions of others. Right now, Clare hoped she had sensed someone else's fear or anger.

"Help me move her," Clare said to David.

As they carried Ita to an empty examination table, Clare

realized she'd not seen the two indents who had been with the team.

"Where are Luis and Hal?" Clare asked. A knot hardened in her stomach as she realized the answer before David spoke.

"They're dead," David said flatly.

"Did you even give them a chance?" Kyne growled, his voice booming above the distant thunder.

The indent's presence startled Clare. She spun to see Kyne standing in the doorway. He was animal-quiet, always appearing unexpectedly.

"They had no chance," David said.

Kyne stepped forward. "You worthless–"

He collapsed before he'd covered half the distance, his large frame crumpling to the floor. The implant grafted to his spine had activated when it detected biochemicals associated with hostility; a safety precaution installed by the Ministry of Labor on all indents.

To her surprise, Clare found herself kneeling next to Kyne, pressing two fingers against his throat, checking his pulse.

"Didn't you deactivate the implants, David?"

He exhaled heavily, something between a laugh and a sigh. "No. And I'm sure they're thankful for it."

Archeological records gathered over the years by the different teams on Ceres had pieced together a history of a civilization that had existed nearly four million years. During this lengthy span, the civilization blossomed, developing vast technologies and spectacular megalopolises. Then, somewhere in the last million years, the civilization stagnated. From what could be deciphered of the alien histories, war enveloped the world. It was fought with bioengineered soldiers, living weapons. Weapons that thought; weapons that died.

The war lasted for centuries, until the ability to kill surpassed all other arts. The inhabitants vanished. The great cities crumbled, leaving behind rubble, remnants of Ceres' glory. Complex governments degenerated and divided into primitive tribal groups. The centuries' long war had devastated the planet, exterminating all intelligent beings, leaving only their shadows behind. All of this took place before humanity would venture to the stars, while Earth evolved, humanity blossomed, advancing itself with science.

All of this Clare knew as she searched the database. What she was looking for was a record or a report of an animal matching David's description. But the translated fragments, the archeologists' and the xenologists' records offered little.

The database's AI performed a contextual search, indicating a high correlation between an ancient "living weapon" and the creature. But the AI had based this result more on extrapolation than direct evidence. There were few technical documents existing from the war era, and the most recent data contained supernatural ramblings. The biological weapons, near the end, had become things of worship — gods.

The library door swished open, pulling Clare's attention away from the display. Kyne entered the shadowy room. He moved slowly, warily like a predator sensing a trap.

"I'm glad to see you up," Clare said.

He grunted. "I'm sure you are." The words were slow and measured.

"What David did was wrong," Clare said. "He should have deactivated the implants. I promise he will go before a review board when we return to the Sol system."

"I'm relieved," Kyne said sarcastically. "I'll sleep good tonight." His deep voice sounded like soft, distant thunder itself. Not the rumble of a passing storm, but one approaching.

"I want you to deactivate my implant," he said. "I'm not goin'out like the others. When that thing comes, I want to fight."

Kyne halted a couple meters from Clare, shrouded in shadow.

"What makes you think it's coming?" she asked, uneasy with his proximity. "We don't know anything about it."

Kyne laughed. The sound was loud, bitter, and sharp as a razor. "Ha. It killed. It won't stop now." He stepped closer. "I know exactly how it thinks," his voice growing softer. "I'm an indent, not some aristocrat-hybrid living offworld. My home is Earth in an overcrowded arcology; you get to know killing there." He gestured broadly. "All this is useless. You just need to know what's gonna keep you alive from minute to minute. Nothin' else."

His cold eyes flashed in the shadows, watching her. The storm washed against the building. Kyne shifted in the darkness, revealing half of his stoic face. "It's coming. I know that."

Clare watched the indent for a long moment, listening to the rain. Slowly she retrieved the control pad from her pocket, and thumbed a sequence.

"I'm doing this because I trust in you." Her words were hollow.

As she punched the last digit, the indent lunged forward, bounding the distance in a single, long stride. The swift movement startled Clare. The remote slipped from her hand, clattering to the floor. She lurched back, pressing into the chair with Kyne mere centimeters away. Her heart pounded. His warm breath brushed against her cheek.

Slowly a smile eased onto his lips. "Just testing."

"Step back," Clare fought to keep her voice calm.

Kyne edged away, eyes locked on her. "Maybe you want to reactivate it now?" He inched backward toward the door. "Maybe you feel safer with one more indent snack to offer that thing out there?"

"Shut up!" Clare screamed. "I don't intend to stand by while it kills–" she caught herself.

Kyne stepped through the doorway, pausing momentarily. "Hmm. I wonder how you'll feel when it gets here?"

They watched on a monitor as the creature eased out of a tangle of underbrush, strutting across the tarmac. Six stalk-like legs carried the large, ovoid body that was easily sixteen feet in diameter. Two pair of thick appendages extended from a black, pulpy band where the upper and lower carapaces converged. The creature somewhat resembled a gigantic crab. Occasionally, a brilliant flash of lightning revealed the creature's globular eyes, glistening in the growing dusk. Below the mass of eyes was a circular maw, filled with protruding teeth.

"How did it find us?" David asked.

"It must somehow be able to sense the shuttle's exhaust,"

Clare said half-heartedly, fearing he possessed an ability similar to Ita's Talent.

The creature approached the shuttle in a sidelong-gait, pausing occasionally to extend its leathery appendages as if to sniff the air. As it moved, the audio sensors reproduced the *clicking* sound its crab-like legs made on the hardened tarmac. The noise was barely audible above the sizzling rain.

"I wonder if we can communicate with it?" Clare said. "If we used the first-contact AI, maybe we. . . ?"

"We're not going to try," David said harshly. "That *thing* attacked us yesterday. I'm not in the mood to chat with it."

Clare watched as the creature danced over the tarmac, passing behind the shuttle. "I'm not going to hunt it down and kill it," she said.

She was weary of Ceres, weary of the ceaseless rain and all the problems. She knew David was right — Kyne was right — the creature didn't come here looking for conversation.

"We'll watch it, and stay clear," she said finally. "The supply freighter should arrive any day now. Until then, we'll avoid contact of any type."

As she spoke, she watched the crab-like legs shifting behind the shuttle.

✱ ✱ ✱

Each impact shook the hangar.

"There's no way of knowing when that thing will break through," David said, checking the readout on the mini-railgun. The magazine counter displayed a full bar. "The hangar door is plasteel. But with enough force it will snap like a ceramic pot."

"I know that," Clare said, doing her best to remain in control of the situation. Panic would only make things worse. "There is no way I'm opening that door to shoot, and I'm not sending one of us out there."

"It doesn't have to be one of *us* . . ." David fell silent as Kyne entered the hangar. A MRG slung over his shoulder.

"The other doors are secure," he said, eyeing David. "Go ahead. Don't let me interrupt." Coldness filled Kyne's voice and eyes.

David turned away, hefting his weapon, concentrating on the hangar door.

Kyne moved toward Clare. "So what's the plan?" he asked. "We just stand here and wait until it finds a can opener?"

"You got someplace else to go?" Clare countered. She knew the words cut deeply, and instantly regretted saying them.

Indents were the charge of the Imperial government, until their indenture was served. Kyne could go nowhere without official permission. He didn't get a rotation, nor had the other indents assigned to Ceres. All of them had been on the planet for over two years, serving their indenture for crimes against society.

Kyne marched toward the hangar door, turning to face Clare, ignoring David. "The supply ship is due any day now. Why don't we stay in high orbit until then? Let this thing cool off for a while."

"How do we get to the shuttle?" Clare asked.

"Someone get its attention, draws it away from the compound." Kyne's eyes flashed on David, then back to Clare. "We already know it has a taste for indents." A barren smile returned to his face. "I figure it won't be too tough for me to do."

"That's a good idea," David said enthusiastically. "At least that's better than just sitting here."

"The man knows a good plan when he hears one," Kyne said. "What do you say, boss?"

"I'm not leaving Ita and Kesin," Clare replied.

Kyne's expression soured. "That's your problem. If you want to bring them, then you better have them loaded by the time I get back."

Clare studied the indent. A million thoughts flashed through her mind, each an excuse to agree, each a justification for the risk Kyne was willing to take. She was exhausted, and wanted just to get off the planet.

"Pack the medical supplies," Clare said, turning to David. "We'll move Kesin and Ita to gurneys. Kyne, you wait at the dorm entrance. I'll usc the intercom to tell you when we're ready."

Without waiting for a response from either man, Clare exited the hangar.

* * *

Clare and David worked quickly, transferring their unconscious comrades to the gurneys, locking the medication synthesizers and status monitors in cages below. The shuttle had a minimal medical facility, but enough to keep the two patients stable until help arrived.

"Do you trust him?" David asked in a hushed voice.

Clare thought about the question. She wasn't sure she did trust Kyne, but she was no longer sure if she completely trusted David either. He seemed too willing to agree with Kyne's offer, even though she made the decision.

"We have to," she answered.

After securing Ita and Kesin, Clare went to the intercom.

"We're ready," she said.

David rested his MRG on the gurney alongside Kesin's sleeping form.

"You've got maybe five minutes, maybe less," Kyne answered.

"Let's go." Clare said, grabbing Ita's gurney and pushing it into the corridor with David trailing behind.

In moments they were at the hangar. The battering had stopped; now, only the relentless slap of rain sounded in the large room. For the first time since she'd been on Ceres, Clare was happy to hear the rain.

Without hesitation, she disengaged the door lock, and opened it.

David waited in the corridor with the gurney in front of him like a shield.

Anxious to move, Clare pushed her burden forward as the hangar door climbed upward.

"Come on!" she called.

The hiss of the rain grew louder as the door raised. Clare leaned forward, squeezing herself and the gurney through the widening gap.

Water from the sky bombarded her, popping against her poncho, splashing on the tarmac. She moved fast, halting only when she'd reached the shuttle. Quickly she punched the entry code. Pistons sighed as the shuttle door slowly parted.

David waited in the hangar.

As the bottom half of the door settled, Clare waved to David. She didn't call out, fearing the sound might attract the creature's attention. But her frantic gesturing did little to goad the man forward. Instead, he hefted the MRG, scanning the surrounding jungle from the safety of the hangar.

Clare pushed the gurney up the ramp. Rage burned inside her, fueled by David's cowardice. As she locked Ita's gurney into place at the back of the shuttle, she heard the whine of an MRG.

A scream followed the weapon's report. A cold ball formed in her stomach.

At the shuttle's door, she stood frozen, watching as the creature effortlessly stalked backward, dragging David's lifeless body with one of its appendages planted in his chest. Its legs shifted up and down with a machine-like rhythm as it vanished into the dense foliage.

"He lost it," Kyne said, suddenly stepping from the shuttle's underbelly. "He left the hangar without the prize. He shoulda brought the body along. Then left it behind while he made a run for it. Like he did with Luis and Hal."

The indent hunkered down next to the ramp. This time, Kyne's stealthy appearance didn't startle her. Fear and disgust fused into one awful, nauseating emotion that deadened her to everything else.

Without a word, Clare marched down the ramp. A hard determination filled her as she strode toward the hangar.

"I wouldn't do that," Kyne called. "That thing has a big appetite."

Clare halted, spinning to face the indent. "What the hell am I supposed to do? Leave him there?"

"For a start. Then put the shuttle in orbit and wait for the supply ship."

"No!" Clare yelled, continuing onward.

The creature slid from the jungle, bloated appendages waving in the air as it bounded forward on its crab-like legs toward Clare. Rain pelted its black carapace, giving it a deep, eerie sheen.

"I told you!" Kyne yelled. He hopped effortlessly onto the

ramp. "I hope you're a fast runner."

Kesin was too far away. Clare couldn't reach him before the creature caught her. Long, terrible seconds passed as she struggled to turn and run back to the shuttle. When she'd reached it, she slammed past Kyne, pushing her way into the cockpit.

With water-shriveled fingers, Clare jabbed at the console, hoping the comlink would detect the sats were offline and switch to a surface broadcast. At this range, she knew a surface signal could cut through the weather. Through the cockpit's viewport, she watched as the hangar door closed.

As though it understood, the creature charged toward the hangar, its bulk moving with preternatural speed in a straight line. Yet it wasn't fast enough. It collided with the plasteel door. The collision sounded with a thunderous *boom*, and the creature stumbled back several meters. In an instant, it hurled its bulk against the hangar again and again, ferocious and determined.

"Persistent," Kyne said from the cockpit, his elbows propped against each side of the bulkhead. Behind him, the shuttle door hissed shut.

Clare punched another code into the console, then she peeled off her poncho and slapped it into the copilot seat.

"I'm not letting it kill Kesin," she said.

Kyne's watched her for a moment as though he were attempting to solve a riddle. There was no warmth or compassion in his visage; rather, a vacuum of emotion that she knew could quickly explode into anger.

"I expect you to help me," she announced after a moment.

"What do you think I can do?"

"Distract it like you did before. And I'll get Kesin."

"Ha! How about *you* distract it, and I get the dead guy on rollers?"

"I don't believe you'll get Kesin," she said. "I don't trust you."

"But you trust me to distract that thing?"

"I don't have a choice. And you don't have one either. If we don't get Kesin, I won't release the security lockdown on the shuttle. Either all of us leave, or none of us."

"So you'd sacrifice sleeping beauty back there—" Kyne motioned toward Ita— "if I refuse to help?"

His dark eyes settled on Clare; his gaze burned through her as though he could see her very soul.

"Or maybe you just want to lose me?" he said. "Keep the creature on my trail while you get into orbit. Is that it?"

"That's not it!" Clare screamed, pushing past him. "I'm not leaving anyone."

She activated the shuttle's medical monitor and connected Ita's med-sensors. The notion of removing Ita's sedative flicked through her mind. But she quickly dismissed it, knowing it would take too long for the drugs to wear off, and even then Ita would probably be hysterical and useless.

"Let me get this straight," Kyne said. "Everyone's life is in my hands?" An icy smile solidified on his lips. "I have to say, I enjoy the irony."

"Why'd you do it before?" Clare asked weakly. A feeling of shame washed over her as she realized what she was asking of a man she didn't want to stand near.

Kyne moved closer, towering over her. His poncho dripped, clinging to his powerful torso, telling his life's history to the archeologist with a record of physical form and muscle. A life of labor, devoid of compassion and trust.

"I wanted to be free," he said. "That's why I did it. Because I thought I might not come back. Because when you only get a little piece of something, something you know you can't have, you want more." As he spoke, he rubbed the back of his neck with a hand, the spot where the implant was grafted into his spine.

For the first time, Clare saw a crack, a break in his unyielding façade. She heard his words, but recognized the lie. Beneath his callous exterior was a skulking fear, a fear of humanity . . . of kindness. She had deactivated his implant. She had stopped treating him like an indent. The act was as alien to him as the creature outside.

"When we're picked up," Clare began, her voice low and raspy. "I'll say you're a researcher. I'll say you're David. It'll take a while to figure out otherwise. By then you can be on Mars."

Kyne's eyes locked on her. In his powerful gaze, she saw his wariness, and his desire to believe.

"I have some credits banked–" she lowered her head, embarrassed by her ability to make such an offer. "I don't get much time to spend them. I'll give them to you, so you can hitch a ride to a colony world on the frontier. No one could trace you there."

Kyne stepped back, his countenance dark and sullen. "So I get the creature to chase me around the compound a couple of times and you buy me a new future? Is that the deal?"

Clare nodded, a slow and weary motion.

"You got a deal," he said. "I always thought I'd make a good farmer."

His heavy-booted feet clanked against the shuttle's plating as he moved toward the door. "Let's do it now." He glanced at Clare, flashing a quick smile. "I don't like long waits."

As the shuttle's ramp lowered, creature scuttled along the length of the hangar door, as though it were looking for an opening, probing for a weakness, ignoring all else.

Kyne took one step onto the ramp, as though testing the surface.

"We don't have much time," Clare said. Above them the dark mantle of night descended upon Ceres.

The indent made no reply. Instead, he reached beneath his poncho and removed a monoblade. The device was used like a machete to cut thick vegetation. Its edge, honed to a single atom allowed it to slice through most any material.

"When it clears the tarmac, I'll get Kesin," Clare said. "I'll need a few minutes."

Kyne shifted his attention from the creature to Clare. The wary, predatory alertness had returned. Clare felt her face begin to flush.

"Don't leave without me," he said.

Quickly the indent bolted down the ramp, gaining speed as he hit the tarmac.

The motion attracted the creature. In an instant, it scampered after the indent, legs *clacking* against the hard surface.

As Kyne bounded into the dark mass of vegetation, the monoblade slashed at the twisted undergrowth. The creature trailed on his heels, its large mass easily slipping through the tangled growth.

When both had vanished from sight, Clare dashed into the cockpit. Hurriedly her fingers worked at the keys, moving through selections as she opened the hangar door and engaged the autopilot prep sequence. The shuttle's engines rumbled to life; preflight displays winked on and scrolled across cockpit monitors.

Clare hit the tarmac at a full run. The hangar door climbed upward, and inside laid Kesin, motionless on the gurney.

Water splashed as Clare's boots slapped the tarmac. She slowed her pace, grabbing the gurney, and then heaved against it, pushing it forward. Her pulse roared in her ears, deafening her to everything else.

Time seemed to slow as she moved, giving Clare the feeling she had lived millennia on Ceres, through the rise and fall of its civilization, through the centuries' long war and the ensuing destruction.

Her feet slipped on the wet ramp as she struggled under the weight of the gurney. Time burned away as she maneuvered into the shuttle. Pushing and dragging, she eventually steered the gurney inside. Just as she locked it down, a motion through a viewport caught her attention. She froze.

Meters from where he'd entered the jungle, Kyne emerged in a heated sprint, the creature close behind.

As it cleared the jungle, its pace quickened. In an instant, a long, bloated appendage writhed forward, slashing at Kyne. The thing swept furiously back and forth, only slowing after making contact with a sickening, wet smack.

The powerful blow sent the indent reeling forward, tumbling across the wet tarmac, arms and legs flopping as he rolled.

With ferocious speed, Kyne bounded to his feet, facing the creature. The unending torrent washed a scarlet line down the back of his shredded poncho.

The creature halted before Kyne, its legs dancing in place. Up and down they pistoned, animated by an inhuman malevolence. It sidled in one direction then another, seemingly unsure of its prey's intent.

Clare started down the ramp.

"Stay there," Kyne called. He raised the monoblade, inching forward, deliberate and cautious, an animal ready to attack.

The creature scuttled back from the advance, its legs lowering its bulk as though preparing to spring.

In a blur, Kyne charged, monoblade lifted high. But the attack quickly came to an end as the indent crumpled to the slick black tarmac, unconscious.

Terror and rage squeezed Clare so tightly; she struggled with each breath. Frantically she searched for the remote in her pockets. Confusion tangled her thoughts. How could the implant activate? Could the creature produce some sort of electromagnetic interference?

The alien beast shifted its position, cruel, slithering black appendages reaching forward. Reaching for its motionless prey.

Without hesitation, Clare stormed toward the thing, screaming in rage until her lungs burned with the fire.

The creature balked for a split-second, as though considering the new threat. And just as quickly, the uncertainty vanished. It crouched as Clare approached.

In a sudden, swift movement, Kyne lurched upward. With ease, the monoblade sliced through two of the creature's worming appendages. Black fluid gushed from the severed ends. A long, rising squeal issued forth.

The creature swiftly scuttled away from Kyne, into the gloom of the surrounding jungle, sluicing a trail of black liquid.

Kyne clambered to his feet, and staggered toward Clare.

✳ ✳ ✳

"I did what it expected," Kyne said.

He stood shirtless, braced against the cockpit bulkhead as Clare placed a suture patch over the wound on his back. "I figured it'd seen the other indents go into paralysis, so I did the same. Lured it."

Ceres' sullen surface hung in the corner of the viewport, with the remainder filled by the ebony distances of space.

"You used yourself as bait," Clare said.

"As a trap," Kyne countered.

Clare pressed her thumb against the patch's activation node, activating its nano devices.

"Once we're aboard the supply freighter," Clare said, "you'll need to keep to your cabin as much as possible."

"Why are you doing this?" Kyne asked.

Clare thought a moment, staring out the viewport toward the countless lights in the cold darkness of space.

"When you only have a little piece of something," she said, "sometimes you want more."

THE NAME OF THE ENEMY

CAPTAIN CAYLE BANKS PEERED over the ancient bastion wall, occasionally glimpsing the liquid movement of the alien monstrosities as they squirmed through the beams of moonlight. Hatred burned inside him at the sight of the endless roiling mass.

In the black vault above, countless pyres burned with seeming disinterest. Cayle knew that three of those flickering lights in the firmament were UW cruisers, carrying twenty-five thousand troops. And yet, he and his company were surrounded in a planetside fortress, waiting for their death.

The captain turned from the ugly vista, facing Lieutenant Alina Osborn. She stood near the arching entrance to the citadel, dressed in CAX, waiting for Cayle's orders.

"This is pointless," he muttered, striding toward the lieutenant.

She matched his height, but not his bulk. Still, in her protective ceramite armor exoskeleton, dubbed CAX, her slender form did not speak of weakness. Years of duty had hardened her. In the dim light, Cayle noticed her pallid flesh, and the concern in her dark eyes.

"I share your anger, Captain. But he is a Psi, and the official liaison of the UW. Challenging his authority is as dangerous as fighting crawlers–" she nodded toward the creatures twisting in the darkness.

The 4th Company had been dug-in at pre-United World fortress of Saverne for three days. The invading swarm of aliens had appeared on the world no more than one month prior. While waiting for reinforcements, Cayle had simply been fighting a holding action, waiting for help. Contact from the other elements of the regiment and his CO had ended early in the engagement. He'd ordered his company into Saverne Fortress just as the UW cruisers entered orbit. His first transmission placed him under the command of Malachi Avoric, the Military Liaison for the UW assigned to this world.

"Waiting here serves no purpose," Cayle replied. "All we are doing is allowing those creatures to multiply. With each world they infest, their ability to push through the dimensional barriers grows. Hundreds of thousands of humans died here, and all we do is wait on the word of a Psi. While the crawlers grow stronger, we become weaker. And now a *Natural* has been placed in charge." Cayle spat the last sentence, as though the words themselves were poisonous.

Alina remained silent, her eyes shifting through the shadows beyond. In the distance, hissing and shrill screeches echoed. The malign noises caused her to wince.

"I'm going to speak with him," Cayle suddenly announced.

Alina grabbed his arm as he passed. Her grip was firm, a soldier's grip. The two were close enough to ignore this breach in rank. "Malachi may be a Natural," she said. "But he carries the authority of the UW Council. He may not be interested in the complaints of a captain."

"He needs to hear," Cayle said, shrugging free of her hold, and marching through the archway.

✱ ✱ ✱

Maps and reports covered the gray-black walls of the chamber that served as Liaison Malachi Avoric's headquarters. Tables, chairs, an endless array of computers and communications equipment cluttered the oblong room. Cables snaked across the floor, crisscrossing from one device to another.

Cayle stood in the doorway, waiting for permission to enter, all the while eyeing Avoric.

The man shifted about the congested room gracefully, passing from one display to the next, seemingly comparing the information to a datapad he clasped in one hand. A flurry of personnel attended to their various tasks, ignoring the presence of both Avoric and Cayle.

When the fuse of his patience had burned away, Cayle finally spoke. "Liaison Avoric," he started. "I must discuss our strategy."

Clad in a black uniform with red piping and a UW insignia on the high-cut collar, the man formed what Cayle thought to be the model for a useless bureaucrat.

Avoric ignored the words, eyes shifting over the display on the datapad.

Cayle struck a stance in the doorway, hands locked behind his back, gaze fixed in the distance. He had no intention of leaving.

Eventually, Avoric lifted his head to face Cayle. "I appreciate your concern for *my* strategy, Captain. But your effort is wasted on the matter."

Cayle fought the urge to step forward. Instead he spoke louder. "Liaison Avoric, there are twenty-five thousand troopers waiting in orbit. Why?"

Avoric watched Cayle for a long moment, seemingly non-plused, a man unraveling a puzzle, nothing else. Liaison Avoric approached Cayle.

For the first time, the captain noticed the white of a thin scar snaking from Avoric's ear, down his neck, burrowing into his collar. A cold, almost bleak stare settled in the man's jet eyes.

Like so many Naturals, Cayle thought. *He uses authority to compensate for genetics.*

A genned soldier, Cayle had not fought in the war between the human Naturals and Hybrids. But decades and the uniting of the two types of humans through the creation of the United Worlds Council did little to wash away the deep-rooted animosity. Cayle detested being placed under the command of a Natural. And it was all the more bitter because Avoric was a Psi. Now the captain wondered if the liaison was attempting to read his mind, searching for a psychological edge.

Chatter and activity continued around the two men, undaunted by their subtle confrontation. "The troops descend

ARTIFACTS   **47** when they are ordered to do so," Avoric said flatly. "Your concern does not rest with them. Your task is to maintain the integrity of this fortress until I request reinforcements."

"With troops in orbit, we have enough forces to destroy these creatures," Cayle countered. "With each passing hour that task becomes more difficult, and the cost grows. But then you probably care little for the cost of genned soldiers."

"If you challenge my authority again, Captain Banks, you will be stripped of rank and court-martialed. You do as you're ordered. I require nothing else from you."

Anger festered in Cayle's gut. This Psi possessed a deadly mixture of ignorance and insolence. "What purpose does waiting serve?"

A thin smile cut across Avoric's sharp visage, as though forming a second scar. "It serves my purpose." With that, Avoric departed, wading into the tangle of equipment, eyes again focused upon the datapad. "You are dismissed," he called over his shoulder.

Terentia Galen had worked as a xeno-biologist for the last ten years — the years since the invasion. Like most, her specialty had become the crawlers. The creatures were intriguing, the most unusual lifeforms she'd ever studied. But with so much at risk, she no longer enjoyed the work. From their first appearance, the aliens had been unstoppable and relentless, cutting a swath through the core of the human worlds. This wasn't a war; it was a culling. And now she found herself trapped inside an archaic fortress, surrounded by thousands, if not tens of thousands of those very creatures.

Deciphering their genetics was the task of scientists such as herself. But the *things* were not from this universe, making them difficult to study, and nearly impossible to understand. Though many theories were bantered about, nothing adequately explained how they had so quickly adapted to this universe. Many postulated that the crawlers existed to travel from dimension to dimension, and as a result, adaptation occurred as quickly in them as some animals could alter skin pigmentation to hide in particular environments — the crawlers were genetic chameleons. Others suggested unknown fields and psychic forces that altered the creatures. Most of the theories were more myth than science to her.

"What have you found?" The coarse voice pulled Terentia from her dark broodings. When her mind refocused, she found herself leaning over a crawler corpse, peering at its internal organs.

The crawler stretched nearly eight feet from its visceral hump to the tip of its tentacles, all of which possessed a tenacular club with sinister hooks used for both ambulation and as weapons. Very little bone existed in the alien, except surrounding its small brain and ganglia. It possessed mandibles and a circular oral cavity of rasping teeth that flayed human flesh efficiently. It didn't have eyes; rather, it used psychic energy to perceive its environment.

"Liaison Avoric," Terentia said, clambering from the stool she occupied. "My apologies. I was in thought."

She sensed the Psi's stare upon her. It felt as though he were aware of her every move. He gave no response.

"I . . . I have learned much," she stammered, struggling to report. "Comparison with previous specimens from other worlds shows much mutation and adaptation. They seem to be evolving more rapidly now."

Avoric's head tilted slightly, indicating interest — or perhaps disinterest. He meandered down the length of the dissection table, his pace slow. Deliberate. The gait of a man out for an evening stroll. At various points he halted, inspecting the eviscerated crawler.

Quickly, Terentia moved to his side. "This creature has increased muscle mass in its extremities and mantle. I believe this mutation enhances strength and agility beyond what we have seen in prior specimens. Its lungs are also enlarged, perhaps adapting it to thin atmospheres, and probably preventing fatigue during extensive physical activity."

"Believe . . .?" he stretched the word.

As she uttered the remark, Terentia had regretted it. She was a scientist. Facts were her tools, not opinions and beliefs. "Yes, believe," she replied, rallying. Never did she allow anyone to unsettle her as much as Avoric. "Or speculation, since I have not examined a living specimen."

During the decade Terentia had been studying the crawlers, a greater burden had been placed on xeno-biologists to understand this new threat to humanity. When there were no fast answers, it was the xeno-biologists who were persecuted. But they had not been tampering with the workings of the universe. It had been the psychics, those like Avoric who could peer into the fabric of existence, intermingle thoughts with the laws governing the dimensions, and venture beyond, into other universes, other places that had remained unknown to humanity for millennia. They had bridged the gap. Opened a gateway between this universe and somewhere else, unleashing the monsters that now stalked the human worlds, devouring all life. Now it was her job to find a weakness in this new enemy, and exploit it. Providing a weakness existed, and provided that humanity survived long enough to find one.

"Is that all?" Avoric asked.

"No," Terentia said, noticing something she'd been blind to previously. Fearing she might reveal her suspicions, she tried to direct the conversation elsewhere. "No. This world seems to possess more mutations than the other infested worlds. It's as if there is something here that promotes their change."

"More speculation?"

"Yes."

"When you are finished," Avoric said, gesturing to the racks of specimen containers, "destroy each of these."

"Naturally," Terentia said without hesitation. "I will adhere to the protocols."

She refused to surrender so easily, however. "Do you sense anything unusual about this world?" Terentia asked.

Avoric turned, an arched eyebrow revealing surprise. "Many things. I find this planet makes my subordinates bold."

The xeno-biologist lowered her head, knowing she'd overstepped her bounds. Sometimes she struggled with her curiosity. It had been a part of her genetic template — a necessity for a good scientist. She was bred for her work.

"I apologize," she said. "Because you are a Psi, I thought perhaps you sensed something about this world that brought about mutations. Something unusual."

"Your enthusiasm is noted. But I'm here to gain answers, not provide them. I need you to collect as much data as you can before the counter assault begins."

"I understand," Terentia said.

Avoric had always seemed remote, but now he seem doubly so, and this piqued Terentia's curiosity all the more. The UW's selection of him, and the power he possessed were unusual as well. He was aloof for a Natural and uncommonly dominant among genned humans. For years she had attributed this to his Psi talent — a Natural talent that could not be reproduced through genetic engineering, a gift that prevented the extinction of his kind during the old war. Yet, she sensed something more, something unnatural. There, tugging at her was the answer. It was obvious now, but so obvious that she'd overlooked it before. There was a strange quality to his movements, his actions, his personality, and Terentia recognized their source.

"Liaison Avoric," she said, trailing him to the doorway. "Has crawler DNA been introduced into your biology?"

Avoric halted. Slowly his head lifted, as though appealing to some greater power.

"Are you to study me?" he asked, keeping his back to her.

Terentia stepped away, sensing something about the man, a danger she had never felt previously. "No. It is my nature. I am curious," she said tentatively.

"Make your study of the aliens infesting this world, and not me."

The liaison marched from the laboratory.

Horror seized Terentia, a malignant growth spreading through her mind, throughout her body. She did not need to be a Psi to sense the truth in Avoric's reaction. It came together now. The crawlers could infiltrate a Natural's DNA, such humans did not possess the safeguards against genetic attacks. And how fitting that a Natural Psi be selected. The crawlers also possessed the same Psi abilities, and were drawn to psychic radiations like insects to light.

Hurriedly she retrieved her commlink, selecting Captain Banks's private band.

✱ ✱ ✱

Cayle returned to the balcony, blurting orders into his commlink.

"What's the situation?" Alina asked, approaching Cayle as he arrived. "There's plenty of chatter on the links, but it's encrypted."

The 4th Company numbered fewer than 80 heads, and Cayle was taking every precaution to prevent the loss of any more. With practiced ease, he snapped off his throat-mic. "Terentia Galen, one of Avoric's xeno-biologists, just told me something of interest."

Alina waited patiently, feeling her worry line her face.

"Avoric has crawler DNA mingled with his," he said.

"How?"

Cayle gazed into the thick gloom, attempting to order his thoughts. "The Naturals lost the war between our kinds. We could have destroyed them. But their uncanny Psi talent helped them turn the tables — gave them a bargaining tool. Instead, Hybrids believed they needed the Naturals and their abilities."

Alina listened intently, her hands going through the motions of readying her mini-rail gun.

"You believe he allowed it? What does he have to gain by betraying humanity?" Alina asked, clearly knowing where Cayle was heading. She underscored her question by snapping a clip containing twenty thousand micro-pellets into her MRG. "These creatures are not interested in peace or allies. They are driven by blind instinct. And the destruction of all life seems to be their primary objective."

"Yes," Cayle said. "But it was the Natural psychics who found them, and who opened the portal between the dimensions. Don't you see? Alone the Naturals could not defeat us. But now they have an army that can." The captain pivoted and commenced pacing. "Over the years the Naturals have manipulated the UW Council, placing themselves in positions of power. They've set a trap and lured us into it."

"It doesn't make sense," Alina argued, shaking her head. "Avoric must know these creatures won't stop with Hybrids.

Naturals will be destroyed too."

"Unless *he's* found a way to bargain," Cayle countered. "Terentia believes he can communicate with them. And right now twenty-five thousand reinforcements hang in orbit — " he thrust a hand at the sky — "and Avoric waits. He may no longer be a Natural. Perhaps the crawlers have managed to overcome the Psi, controlling him as their puppet."

"What do we do?"

Cayle looked like a caged animal, locked within the walls of the fortress, unable to lash out. Alina knew that such a betrayal would cut him deeply, plumbing a profound anger inside him.

"We won't be sacrificed," he said, placing his hands upon her shoulders. Even through the CAX she felt his strength. "I need you to take a team and enter the tunnels beneath the fortress. Find an exit, a place clear of the crawlers. Afterward, we'll stealth out, and contact the cruisers ourselves."

"What will you do?" she asked warily. His physical contact made it clear she could go beyond her rank and ask a question rooted deeper in emotion than in tactics.

"I intend to keep the *liaison* occupied until you find a passage out. My absence would draw his attention."

She pulled away from his grip, all business now. Effortlessly she slung the MRG over her shoulder. "If there's a way out, I'll find it."

"Only use encrypted links," Cayle said. "If he asks about it, I'll tell him it is our protocol."

"What about Terentia and the rest of Avoric's staff? How many of them go with us?"

"All of the genned go. The Naturals can stay here," he said coldly.

✳ ✳ ✳

Lieutenant Alina Osborn led a team of five soldiers through the entrance leading into a maze of ancient subterranean tunnels.

"Everyone stay on this band, and keep it crypted," she ordered. A series of confirmations followed.

Alina knew Avoric had the layout of the fortress, but getting them would stir interest. She didn't want to risk accessing the liaison's computers, knowing a chance existed of being detected.

"Iason, take point," Alina said. "The rest keep back and be ready."

The team relied upon night-vision units, using a frequency of light invisible to the human eye, and thought to be invisible to crawlers as well. With the goggles, the stonework tunnels became a blue-gray iridescent world of bisecting passages and smaller secondary shafts.

Iason moved ahead, checking each juncture, tapping on his throat-mic twice to signal "all clear." Not speaking kept the noise to a minimum.

Although she wasn't sure of which path to take, Alina knew which direction she needed to head. So long as the primary tunnel led away from the fortress, she intended to follow it. It was wider than the intersecting passages that seemed to form a honeycombed network, and she knew that in a broader space they would stand a better chance. The crawlers had brute strength and inhuman speed. Many times she'd heard the primordial shriek the creatures made when they set upon a human foe. A crawler never left its prey until the heart stopped beating. They clung to their victims, consuming living flesh, ripping and gnawing to the moment of death. Only then did a crawler lose interest and race onward to the next victim.

"I think I spotted something," Iason whispered over the link.

"Clarify," Alina said.

"Not sure. I saw movement. Maybe a heat ghost or debris."

With a clenched fist, Alina halted the remainder of the team. Iason stood no more than twenty meters ahead, leaning against the concave tunnel wall, hefting his MRG.

"Take up positions on both sides of the intersection," Alina said in a throaty whisper. "No one fires until I order it. I *don't* want a swarm of crawlers down here."

The team divided, two settling low against each wall behind Iason.

The air in the tunnel was thick and damp. Alina took several deep breaths before ordering the scout to move ahead.

Slowly, he peered around the corner, raking the tunnel for any sign of movement. Just as he edged forward, a crawler, black and slick, was upon him. Hooked tentacles flailing, wrapping around his torso, wriggling beneath his CAX, thrashing against the armor's exterior. A furious storm of *snapping* hooks and *snicking* mandibles.

Iason tried to speak, his words coming over the link as a thick gurgling. A piercing screech issued from the crawler as it tore flesh and cracked bone.

"Fire!" Alina yelled.

In an instant, a maelstrom of micro-pellets penetrated the human and monster tangled in a deadly knot. The MRG's magnetic rail hummed softly, as the whine of high velocity, one hundred rounds per-second projectiles sliced the air.

Stone sparked as the pellets ricocheted, bouncing down the tunnels, dancing from floor to ceiling to walls. Iason and the crawler shuddered, momentarily held aloft by the unrelenting stream of firepower. Then the two quickly dissolved, collapsing, and spilling onto the hard floor.

Once the firing had ceased, the familiar scuttle and *clacking* sound filled the passage. Hooked tentacles whirling through the air, slapping against the stone to gain purchase, pulling the crawlers forward.

"Fall back!" Alina ordered.

As the team retreated, a flood of creatures poured around the junction from the direction the first had appeared. The floors, walls and ceilings glistened with the fearsome monsters.

Now the soldiers operated on training and genned instinct. Two tossed phosphorus grenades, the remainder fired upon the ensuing swarm.

The tunnel exploded in a flash of burning chemicals. Crawlers sizzled, and those attempting to push through suffered the same fate. MRGs fired continuously, liquefying the creatures as they writhed and struggled forward.

✹ ✹ ✹

"Captain Banks, the crawlers are breaching the outer wall!"

"Pull your platoon inside the citadel," Banks ordered Lieutenant Kian. "We'll hold there."

Cayle switched his commlink to First Sergeant Hanson's band, he was commanding Alina's platoon. "Pull back. We need everyone in the citadel now. The perimeter is compromised."

Cayle desperately wanted to link Alina, but he thought better of it. She'd contact him when she could.

"It appears the moment arrives," came Avoric's voice.

Cayle spun, keeping to the balcony wall. From his perch he had been observing the courtyard below.

The captain deliberately raised his MRG, pointing at Avoric.

"You intend to shoot me?" The liason asked wryly.

Numerous options played through Cayle's head. He grew weary of the cat and mouse game, and now it appeared the Psi had made the first move. He couldn't risk Avoric flooding his mind with psychic noise. His finger went to squeeze the MRG's trigger. But his finger didn't move.

"You seem more anxious to kill me than the enemy," Avoric said, waving into the night. As he spoke, an eerie chorus of *clicks* and squeals filled the air. Without looking, Cayle's mind filled with the image of crawlers cascading into the courtyard.

"You've betrayed humanity," Cayle said.

"Do you mean all of humanity, or just one kind?" As he spoke, the liaison padded toward the wall, looking over the edge.

Invisible chains locked Cayle in place. Rage coursed through his body with every heartbeat.

"You seem ready to sacrifice Naturals," Avoric said dryly. "Would the same ease come with Hybrids?"

The recon team bolted through the tunnel, the foul reek of burning flesh thick in the air. Alina vocalized the command to link with Cayle's private band.

"Captain, Lieutenant Osborn here. The crawlers have entered the tunnels and are advancing."

She raced to the entrance, not looking behind. Doing so would only slow her.

"Captain Banks," she repeated into her link.

An oily shadow darted past her. Before she could focus, a crawler slapped against Julian, throwing him to the tunnel floor. He hit hard, his MRG sliding from his grasp, rattling across the scarred bricks. With genned speed, he pulled his blade. It flashed as it whipped back and forth.

"Move! Move!" Alina ordered to the others.

To break her momentum, she slammed into the wall, spinning with the impact. In a second, she was back on her feet and on top of the crawler lashing at Julian's CAX.

Knowing the MRG would kill both human and monster, she slung it. Instead, she reached down, impaling her armored hand deep into the pulpy mass of the crawler. The hardened ceramite gauntlet pushed through the creature's rubbery skin with an audible rip.

The crawler hissed as though warning Alina away.

Shifting her hand in the thing's body, she felt for the protective bone encasing the brain.

Julian sliced with the blade. A blue viscous ichor seeped from the crawler, but the monster did not relent. Tentacles slapped, and hooks bit into the ceramite armor exoskeleton.

Then Alina found it; a solid mass in her hand. She vocalized a command to her CAX processors, causing her arm and fist to become rigid.

The tightening grip caused the creature to squeal. The sound resounded off the tunnel walls. But Alina found this noise to be pleasant. With a yank, she hefted the crawler from Julian's body. Hooked tentacles held fast to the folds of armor.

"Die now," Alina said, and then clenched her fist into a tight ball. The crawler jerked, shuddered, hissed once again, and then dangled lifelessly in her cold grasp.

✳ ✳ ✳

The warning from Alina buzzed in his ear. Focusing his will, he pushed against the unseen power holding him.

"They can sense us," Avoric said. "Or perhaps taste is more accurate. We produce psychic energy that draws them to us."

Captain Banks, if you receive this, we are sealing the tunnel doors. But that won't hold the crawlers for long, Alina's voice sounded from Cayle's earpiece.

"Why are you in league with them?" Cayle asked, desperately searching for a new tactic, some way to distract the Psi long enough to kill him.

The whine of MRGs rose from below. The crawlers had reached the citadel. Soon they'd come streaming from beneath as well. The retreat from the courtyard played in the captain's mind as though he were watching it through his own eyes.

"They do not understand fear," Avoric continued, ignoring Cayle's efforts. "It is a vestigial emotion in them. It serves them no purpose. I understand that. For an unfathomable time, they have ventured from one world to another, from one galaxy to another, from one universe to another, spanning dimensions, leaving a wake of death. They are driven by desire alone. I've seen the destruction of entire universes in their memories. Each time, they wait for a new threshold to open, ushering them into a new realm to annihilate. It is as if they've found a way to avoid the end of time, evolving to shift from destruction to creation."

"And your kind brought this plague upon us," Cayle said bitterly.

Alina charged forward, gathering her platoon and redeploying them along the interior of the citadel's entrance hall. The barrel-vaulted ceiling spanned over one hundred meters in height. Ornate wood decorated the walls, and polished stone served as a floor.

One by one the squads formed.

The tremendous ceramite gates at the front of the hall groaned as the crawlers massed, their bulk threatening to shatter it.

"Lieutenant Osborn," came Kian's voice. "My platoon is formed at the rear of the citadel. The crawlers are burrowing through the stone. I'll send word when I must drop back."

"Kian, can you contact Captain Banks?"

"Negative. He ordered us inside, and I've had no word since."

Damn, thought Alina.

Soldiers piled tables and chairs in a line, hunkering down behind them.

"We fire on my word," Alina broadcast to her platoon. "Launch grenades and follow with raking fire. We need to choke them at the entrance."

One by one each squad replied, acknowledging her order.

Now the frenetic scratching of hooks and mandibles filled the hall. Soon cracks streaked across the ceramite like ice preparing to burst. A low grinding sound reverberated throughout the large chamber. The timbre deepened until the huge gates burst, sending shards flying through the air, clattering across the floor.

As though a giant shovel had been upended, a writhing mass of crawlers spilled into the hall. They scampered across the polished surface, hissing and screeching. When hooks found no hold on the stone, they slithered and scrambled over each other, all in a blind lust to reach their goal.

"Fire!" Alina shouted.

The solitary word garnered immediate response. Grenades exploded, MRGs fired thousands of rounds into the wave of gangly attackers. And still the crawlers continued.

✳ ✳ ✳

"If you mean me as a natural creation of this universe, then . . . yes, perhaps I am responsible. But it was the same desire to expand that taught us to open the portals between universes. It seems that even a Hybrid does not have that desire excised."

"What do you want? Revenge? Or have you become so much like them that you crave human blood?"

"I want to awaken that vestigial emotion," Avoric said, turning to Cayle. "I want them to remember fear."

"So you mixed your biology with theirs? How does that help to bring them fear?"

Avoric stepped forward, fixing his eyes upon the captain. "I needed to let them sense me above other humans. I needed to communicate. I can feel their desires, and when I allow it, they can sense mine."

Flames blazed in the courtyard, producing large, inhuman shadows on the stony walls. In the distance, Cayle heard the sound of dropships. *The troops*, he thought. *They are here.*

"Humanity cannot continue the war in this manner," Avoric said. "It is a losing proposition. I intend to awaken fear in the crawlers and wage a new war against them. No longer will we flee and hide like whimpering animals."

Attack craft streaked through the blackness above, firing incendiary missiles. Explosions shook the huge fortress. The night now glowered a dull red as fires burned. Smoke streamed, carried by the updraft, blotting out the stars.

Cayle suddenly jerked forward, no longer in the grasp of an unseen hand. Quickly he aimed his MRG at Avoric, but this time it was his own will that stayed his finger.

"You have a battle to fight, Captain," Avoric said, already departing. "And a war to win after that."

The roar and rumble of combat joined the sickening stench of burning flesh. MRGs whined in a glorious chorus. Cayle made his way to the wall, watching the scene unfold. Drop-ships descended from orbit by the hundreds. Soon the crawlers would be destroyed. The image of their death flicked through his mind.

Captain Banks entered the chamber where the UW Liaison waited. Sunlight sliced through the tall windows lining the room, providing a perfect view of the spaceport. Avoric watched as transports lifted to the sky, engines roaring. Cayle stood near the doorway, Lieutenant Alina Osborn at his side. The captain waited for the liaison to acknowledge him.

Transports continued to launch, climbing through the atmosphere into the space beyond.

Long moments passed with no words exchanged. Cayle intended to wait the man out.

"You desire a meeting, Captain." Not a question, a statement.

"Yes."

The liaison's head tilted upward, following the arc of a transport.

"Liaison Avoric, I've come to make a request. It is informal at present, but with your permission I will make it formal."

"This world is no longer under my jurisdiction, Captain. You need not inquire of me."

"For this I must," Cayle said. "I wish to join your campaign. With your approval, I will request that my company be transferred under your dominion until the resolution of the war."

Avoric laughed, a harsh sound. "That may be decades."

"I understand."

"You desire to be placed under my command?" Avoric asked. "A UW Liaison?"

"Yes."

"Such a thing is unusual. And it is so for a reason," Avoric said. "Imagine the fear inspired by a human of my talents and a genned force under his command." The liaison turned from the window, his eyes gleaming. "Such a combination would generate much distrust."

"I can't see how that differs from the present situation," Cayle said. "I am bred for battle, but I can still see truth, and so can those who serve under me. The war you wage is the one I wage."

Avoric gazed at Cayle for several minutes, then returned to the window.

"Captain Banks, I told you that I wanted to rekindle a forgotten emotion in the crawlers. To do that, I require unquestioning dedication. Do you honestly desire to place yourself in such a position?"

"Yes," Cayle quickly replied. "I too want to awaken fear in our enemy. And the name of that fear is humanity."

Liaison Avoric watched another transport stream into the sky. "You may place the formal request with your superiors, Captain."

"Thank you, Liaison Avoric."

"Dismissed."

Cayle turned to leave with Alina at his side. But as he spun, he glimpsed the pale reflection of Avoric upon the window. The captain's keen eyes discerned a thin smile playing upon the man's sharp face. Cayle smiled as well.

ALL BUT FORGOTTEN

A DEEP RUMBLE VIBRATED through Beatrice Station's hull as the alloy skeleton shifted, compensating for external changes in atmospheric pressure. Flat clanks and dull pings sounded from the composite exterior as debris, carried by the Phyra's infernal winds, continually collided with the survey station's composite exterior.

"Doesn't look like much," Rif said. Rif and Liam stood at the side of the cleansing tank, watching the overhead display, waiting for Mehgan to speak.

Rif was short with a bulky, well-muscled form. Stringy, dark blond hair and coveralls stained the red of Phyra's soil gave her an undeserved, grimy appearance.

"It looks like heaven," Mehgan finally said, studying the data on the display.

"Is it a good idea to scan and cleanse it without cataloging it first?" Liam asked.

"Seems good to me," Mehgan replied. "Rif, did you date it for our new assistant director?"

Two months, Liam felt, should be long enough for the shine to wear off the "new assistant director."

"It's kinda hard to get an exact number with the conditions out there," Rif said hesitantly. "The prelim puts it around sixty million years."

"Old enough," Mehgan said. Her gaze dropped from the overhead to Liam. "I've been cataloging for two decades," she said flatly, "and I don't have the patience to catalog another thing."

Lean and weary, Mehgan wore the same coveralls as Rif and the other techs, something Liam had originally thought unusual for a survey station director. She was tall and kept her black hair knotted behind her head. Her blue eyes were lined, and lacked the brightness Liam suspected they once possessed.

"All the more reason to approach it slowly," Liam replied. Another clang on the exterior hull.

"Where did you find it?" Megan asked Rif.

"Sector 410, which we started last week. Right on the edge of the first pass." The tech shifted around the tank. She halted before a wall and tapped it twice with a stubby finger.

The white wall blurred, and then resolved into the image of a surface contour map, overlaid with a green grid. The map formed in perfect alignment with Rif's less-than-average height.

Liam knew that many of the techs had trained the Sensewalls to respond to physical and verbal commands. But he was surprised to see that Rif had trained this one to understand the context of a conversation. It had been listening, and knew what she'd wanted to display.

The Sensewall used a high density, neural-node array to memorize basic instructions. A photosynthetic membrane protected the array, allowing it to sense vibrations, both physical and audio, and to change pigmentation to interact with humans. They were also capable of producing sound, making them the station's intercom system. Most people considered Sensewalls nothing more than smart constructs, or pets at the most. But, when linked with Beatrice, the station's autonomous Created Intellect, a Sensewall could be used to access vast amount of stored information. Obviously Rif had trained it to do just that.

"The crawler found it here," she pointed. It was buried in igneous rock, so it's got to be pretty tough to last this long with all of the activity on Phyra."

An alarm wailed in the garage as Beatrice prepared to close the storm shutters.

"Getting close," Rif added coolly. Like a seasoned solider at ease with the havoc on a battlefield, Rif calmly anticipated the approaching fury of the storm.

Liam hated the storms, and he hated the relentless noises

the station made as the burning winds lashed against its hull. During the last four months he'd found himself wondering if there was enough archeologist left inside him to stay on-site. He continuously found himself mired in political debates more than scholarly matters. He feared that the growing hatred was slowly seeping into his soul, hardening him, making him bitter. Maybe more like Mehgan, he wondered.

Phyra was one of the planets in the Ce'kihn-Human Agreement. It was uninhabitable — which was probably the reason it was ceded to the human Hegemony. With a dense, exotic atmosphere, and a searing heat that baked its surface ceaselessly, structures on Phyra were in need of constant maintenance, and their upkeep needed CIs like Beatrice to manage them. Many scholars in the Hegemony believed that the Ce'kihn had long ago stripped the world of all useful artifacts, leaving behind only insignificant rubbish. Now humanity searched the surface like hungry dogs hoping for a forgotten morsel.

"Clarification complete," Beatrice announced. "Molecular sterilizer purged."

The door to the cleansing tank slid open, revealing a spherical shape, glistening like a pearl.

Mehgan peered inside. "Looks organic, doesn't it?"

"Sorta looks like an egg," Rif said.

Mehgan tapped a button on the tank's console and the holding platform raised. "It seems to have a Ce'kihn style interface port on the side," she said, lifting the artifact from its sling. There was a tired excitement about her. Liam wondered how many years Phyra had taken to burn away her spirit to the point of looking tired on the threshold of a discovery.

Rif stepped closer, examining the alien object. "What if it's some kind of Ce'kihn garbage? Something dumped back before they let us have the world?" She pointed at an opening in the object. "That looks a lot like one of their interfaces."

"You said the preliminary dating placed it around sixty-million years old," Mehgan said. "The Ce'kihn weren't interstellar then."

Frustrated, Liam finally piped in. "We are ignoring several levels of protocol here. I'm just as curious as everyone else, but should we risk damaging it just because we're in a hurry?"

"Can you build-up a connector that will connect it with Beatrice?" Mehgan asked Rif, ignoring Liam. "If there's data inside, I want to extract it—" she turned to Liam —"*before it's damaged.*"

She handed the artifact to Rif, then moved toward the lab's exit. "Come with me, Liam. We need to discuss protocol."

✳ ✳ ✳

Liam followed Mehgan through the station's narrow corridors, halting in the control room.

"Sit if you like," she said, dropping into one of the polyfoam chairs.

The storm shutters around the control room hadn't closed yet, leaving the surface of Phyra visible through the composite windows. Ruddy dust particles blew through the poisonous atmosphere of the small world, making it look as though the station were at the bottom of an sea of red sand. Occasionally a scattering of pebbles collided with the transparent composite, tapping as if anxious to enter.

"Twelve years I've worked this site," Mehgan started. "Twelve pointless years." She spun the chair to face the crimson sea of blowing sand outside. "I was transferred here because of my insubordinate attitude." A quiet laugh followed her words. "Difficult to imagine, isn't it?"

"Mehgan…"

"Let's try following protocol now," she interrupted. "I'm the survey director, I'll talk first."

Liam locked his hands behind his back and waited.

"We are all but forgotten here, condemned for our bureaucratic sins. Nine months on and three off, that's the form of our punishment. In a few years, your three months off-site will become a purgatory, a limbo, where you do nothing but wait, dreading your return to this hell. Rock isn't the only thing windswept on this world, Liam."

He approached the console. "That's why we should be careful . . .," he said. "If we have a find here, then the entire team is boosted off-site, right?"

"Right," she said, an edgy weariness coloring her voice. Her gaze was fixed upon the station's shuttle hangar in the distance.

The pall of dust had lessened enough to see the looming structure that contained the cargo shuttle. Slowly, huge monotanium alloy shutters slid into place like a gigantic gauntleted hand, slowly inching from beneath the surface, buttressing the hangar, protecting it from the encroaching storm.

"And if we're cautious, follow protocol, and send the artifact back to Alexandria, we'll get word in a year or two — providing it's not an alien analog for a apple pie recipe or Ce'kihn trash. And what do you think that wait will do to everyone on station? All we have is hope of leaving. Two years is too long." She paused a moment. The deep groaning of the station and the scratching of sand against the exterior filled the space. "Two years is too late."

Turning her gaze from the disappearing hangar, Mehgan faced Liam. "Archeology isn't a science in the Hegemony. We're centuries behind the Ce'kihn. This is a business . . . not a race. We lost the race long before humans built the first city on Earth."

"But *we* are scientists."

She shook her head. "No. Maybe you are now, but you won't be in a few months. Erosion works fast on this world."

A low hum filled the chamber as the storm shutters closed around the control room. Dark gray slabs of metal slid from beneath the port, little by little, blocking the stormy world beyond.

"You don't have to be a part of this, Liam. Maybe you still have the chance at a career, the rest of us don't. My advice is to stay in your quarters until we're done. If we screw up, you can honestly say you weren't involved."

"And if it turns out to be a hit?" Liam asked.

"Sometimes risks pay off. If this one does, then we've all paid for our indulgences, and we all get to leave, including you."

The room was cramped, the bunk hard and narrow. Liam closed his eyes, trying not to dwell on the confining space of his quarters and the hellish world where he was trapped. The music he'd selected could barely be heard above the thundering storm.

Memories of the excavation on Jaipur flicked through his mind. The intense heat, thick foliage and the never-ending assault of insects were there. Eight months of digging across the planet's surface with no hits.

"How do you account for the success of the Patel Corp team?" Josef Meinhardt asked — at the time Josef was the site director on Jaipur.

Liam stifled a laugh. "They're corporate gold-diggers, blasting their way across the planet. They don't even know what they're looking for. I wouldn't call any of their hits a success. More like a tragedy. Think of all the knowledge that has been lost in their excavations."

Perspiration glistened on Josef's puffy face. His eyes were dark stones without a shine.

"Patel is very careless, true," Josef said finally, his words thick with a central Hegemony accent. "But likewise, maybe we are too cautious." He lifted a viewpad, thumbing through displays before handing it to Liam. "The department head has decided to transfer you to another site."

The news had been anticipated.

"You have skills that are not being utilized here," Josef continued. "You're being transferred to a site more compatible with your abilities."

At the time Liam had detected a faint satisfaction in Josef's pronouncement. Now he clearly heard it. Something else was there too. Delight.

"...Clen...we need...override," a garbled voice pulled Liam across light-years of space back to Phyra.

He rose and tapped the intercom. "This is Liam, can you repeat?"

"...to the garage. We...to override the local controls." The voice was fuzzy with static, but it sounded like Rif.

"Rif?" he said. "There is something wrong with–"

His words were pushed aside by the blare of the station's General Quarters alarm. At least that's what he thought it was. While traveling to Phyra, he'd memorized the alarms, though he hadn't planned on hearing them first hand.

He yelled into the intercom. "I'm on my way!"

✳ ✳ ✳

Liam scrambled through the narrow corridors, hurriedly ducking low hatchway as he ran. A deep rumbling swallowed the cry of the alarm as he neared the garage.

The garage ceiling was the tallest point in the station, vaulting high to accommodate the large excavation machinery housed there. This structural requirements made it susceptible to high-speed wind.

As Liam entered, the huge space resonated with noise. A high-pitched keening sounded above the rest of the cacophony — like thousands of voices crying in torment.

Rif hurried to Liam.

"What's going on?" Liam had to shout to be heard over the din.

The station's techs were latching down the crawlers and pressure containers.

"Beatrice is having a seizure," Rif said. "She's lowered the garage shutters, and we can't raise 'em." Rif gripped his arm with surprising strength and guided him toward the control island at the center of the garage. "You have to do a local override. Beatrice isn't responding."

"Where's Mehgan?" Liam asked.

Rif shook her head.

"Wouldn't it be safer to sedate Beatrice and get control of her autonomic processes?"

"Yeah, it *would*," Rif snapped. "But we don't have time. This storm's gonna rip us apart if we don't get those shutters up."

Liam studied the controls, hesitant to proceed with the override. Like scanning the artifact, this might be another unnecessary risk. But there was little time to consider other options.

"Hurry," Rif barked.

Then the choice was made; thoughts and memories whirled around his mind in a storm of their own. He listened to the growling wind and the groaning hull. There was only one way to escape the whirlwind that had engulfed him.

He started to speak, but realized there was too much noise for voice activation. Instead he punched the authorization code on the keypad, and he placed his thumb over the lock, waiting for his DNA to validate the override.

Long seconds passed.

"You *do* know the code?" Rif shouted.

Liam nodded. "Yes. But it's not working."

"Try again."

As he re-entered the code, another sound joined the roar. Metal grating, rending somewhere near the top of the garage. A second alarm blasted.

"Forget it!" Rif shouted. "The hull's ruptured. Atmosphere's bleeding in."

"Can you fix it?" Liam asked.

The other techs scrambled from the garage.

"Not right now. We have to go."

By the time they'd reached the corridor, Liam's lungs burned.

Rif pulled a lever and the pressure door rapidly sealed, muffling the noise beyond.

"Will that hold?" Liam nodded at the door, trying to swallow fiery gasps of air.

"Nope," Rif answered, hunching over, settling her hands on her knees. "It'll buy us some time, though. With the garage shutters down and Beatrice gone nutty, this place won't hold together long."

"We'd better get everyone into pressure suits then," Liam said.

"Everyone with a brain is already doing that." She deliberately grinned. "Protocol, you know."

"Then get the crew to the hangar. Maybe we can ride-out the storm there. Is it possible to close the underground airlocks and isolate the station?"

"Yep." Rif said.

The alarms silenced and darkness washed over them. A split-second later the emergency lighting activated, staining everything in a wan, reddish glow.

"I'm going forward to find Mehgan," Liam said. "I'll meet you at the hangar."

✳ ✳ ✳

In the lab, Liam found Mehgan slouching in a chair, unconscious. A cable jacked into the neural interface just behind her ear stretched to a dataport on the console before her. The artifact rested in the sling, another cable connected it to a dataport.

Liam rushed into the chamber, yanking both cables free. He

checked Mehgan's pulse, then her pupils. In the red hue of the emergency lighting her eyes were disturbing voids.

Colors churned and spiraled across the Sensewall, forming patterns. While Liam didn't recognize them, somehow they were eerily familiar. The strange shifting forms pulled at Liam like the gravity of a star on a distant planet. He watched as the blurs solidified, then dispersed. An endless procession of bewildering images tugged at his mind. The world around him began to fade as his thoughts followed the Sensewall's display.

Finally he wrenched his attention away.

"Mehgan," he said, gently shaking her. "Wake up."

She shifted slightly and murmured.

Liam struggled to focus, but the Sensewalls flickering patterns called to him, urging him to look.

"We need to evac," Liam yelled. "Mehgan, can you walk?"

"There's too much," she said faintly. "It's wonderful, but . . . it's unfolding . . . expanding. Too much data for Beatrice. I can't stop it . . . . It is alive, Liam."

Meghan lifted her head, her eyes focusing for a brief moment. "Memories," she uttered. "Never-ending, like a fractal, but alive. Living knowledge . . ." She slumped into the chair.

"The station's tearing apart," he grunted as he hoisted Mehgan in his arms. "And you've made first contact with an unknown alien species. *Great.*"

She mumbled something, though the words made little sense.

Carefully, he pulled the artifact from its harness, and headed toward the hangar airlock.

✳ ✳ ✳

The storm hammered viciously at the station. Even though Liam had sealed the doors behind, the violent thumping and thrashing grew steadily.

He gingerly lowered the helmet of the heavy EV suit over Mehgan's head, sealing it.

The flooring vibrated as Phyra's tempest eviscerated the station's metal body with its scalpel-sharp winds — sand flying at several hundred kilometers per hour, slicing through everything on the station. Hurriedly Liam climbed into his suit.

The station continued to trembled. Metallic cries reverberated through corridors as sections of the structure were furiously ripped away. As Liam reached for his helmet, the ruddy lighting faded into total blackness. Explosions quaked the locker-room. In the darkness, he fumbled the helmet into place.

With a word, the suit's lights illuminated. Next Liam tried the radio, hoping to contact Rif.

Only static hiss.

He grabbed Mehgan's bulky suit and dragged her toward the airlock door. EV suits were heavy, articulated things, designed to protect humans from the pressure of Phyra's dense atmosphere. Casual movement was impossible.

When Liam checked Mehgan's suit monitor, he glimpsed her strangely serene face. It held the dreamy expression of a person witnessing the solution to a sixty-million year old mystery. A tinge of envy touched upon him — what wonders drifted through her mind?

He secured the pack containing the artifact.

With a fierce groan, the locker-room door burst from its hinges, rocketing across the chamber, careening into a wall of lockers opposite. Furious gusts followed as Phyra's atmosphere rapidly filled the area. Burning winds pushed Liam and Mehgan forward, slamming them against the airlock door.

Swirls of red sand clouded his vision. Liam struggled to engage the door's interlock against the powerful gusts. His movements were slow and awkward as though he were moving through a thick fluid, but with the aid of his power-assisted suit, he grabbed the circular interlock handle and twisted.

The door remained sealed.

Again he twisted, turning the interlock in both directions. Still nothing happened. Fear and anger boiled together inside him, distilling into a bleak realization. Without emergency power the airlock door wouldn't open, and walking in the storm was impossible.

"*Suit,*" he ordered, trying to remain calm. "Activate Comm."

"Already active." So much for calm, he thought.

"Rif, can you hear me?"

While listening for an answer, he kneeled and manually activated Mehgan's radio.

"Rif, this is Liam," he tried again. "I can't open the airlock. Emergency power is off."

No response.

Spirals of sand and debris danced in and out of the EV suit's light. How long? Liam wondered.

He tapped Mehgan's faceplate. "Still there?"

His light flooded her helmet. Eyes fluttered, not those of a person sleeping, rather like someone watching a vid.

"Liam, are you receiving me?" The transmission was prickly with static. For a brief moment he thought it was Mehgan speaking. Then he recognized the voice.

He pushed to his feet, the servos in the EV suit working to maintain his balance. "Rif? Where are you?"

"The storm's steppin' all over our comms. So if you lose me, be ready to get through the airlock fast."

"I can't open it," Liam answered. "Power's out–"

"I know," she interrupted. "I'm going to raise it with a portable lifter. Just hang on a couple of minutes."

"I will," he said, looking around the damaged locker-room. "But I don't know if anything else will."

Through a heavy curtain of blowing sand, Liam could see the door slowly inch upward.

He waited for the gap to widen enough, then pushed Mehgan through it.

"She's unconscious," Liam said. "We'll have to carry her."

Several suited hands grabbed Mehgan, pulling to the other side of the airlock.

"Kev and Netter are with me," Rif said. "You hurt? Can you walk?"

"I'm all right."

Once Mehgan cleared the opening, Liam scuttled through.

Rif tapped his helmet. "The access tunnel is already equalized, and the hangar has its own generator so we'll be fine in there until this monster passes." She motioned to Mehgan who was being carried by the other techs. "How bad is she?"

"I don't know. Does the shuttle have a cryo-bed?"

"Yes." Even this close the radio was choppy.

"We'll put her there until our rescue arrives."

* * *

The brilliant stars, swathed in the vastness of space, filled the shuttle's fore viewport. In silence, Liam gazed at the shining specks. A universe filled with countless mysteries.

Once the storm had faded, Rif had activated the shuttle's autopilot. Kilometers above Phyra the craft now orbited, safe from the planet's fury. There were plenty of supplies to last until help arrived. Already a warpspace beacon carried the message across the galaxy.

"Can'ya see the storm?" Rif asked, entering the bridge. Even in zero-gee, the stocky tech had no difficulty in moving about. With a single push she propelled herself toward an empty seat.

Liam glanced away from the ochre world below. He wasn't sure why, but he was embarrassed to be caught daydreaming. Or stardreaming. "No," he said. "It's moved beyond the terminator."

Strapping in, Rif asked, "Think Mehgan'll be okay?"

The images on the Sensewall fluttered through Liam's mind, as if in answer to Rif's question. An incomplete answer. "I think she'll be fine. I'm sure they'll help her back at Luna."

A narrow smile stretched Rif's lips. "I hope so." After a moment, she added, "I won't miss this place. Think they'll rebuild it?"

"No," Liam said. "I believe Mehgan found what the Ce'kihn have been hiding from humanity — a lifeform of living knowledge. For sixty-million years it has been buried on Phyra, waiting — hoping — for someone to find it. I'd bet that humanity just tied the technological race."

Rif starred at him quizzically.

"I'm guessing everything inside that artifact is now inside Mehgan's head," he clarified. "And I have a feeling that the Ce'kihn got their knowledge from the same source."

"So no more middleman, eh?" Rif grinned, turning to gaze at Phyra. "I wonder what else is buried down there?"

Rusting
Edge

THE SMALL SHIP DRIFTED through the boundless void of space, somewhere near the edge of the Azrael sector. Its life poured from its patchwork hull into the cold vacuum.

Inside the ship's metal skeleton alarms howled.

Devin McCowan moved through the cluttered cargo hold toward the puncture in the *Redeemer*. Atmosphere rushed through the opening, forming an unseen hand of air current inside that tugged at him. Awkwardly, he glided through the hold, around crooked towers of salvaged items and countless piles of ragged and damaged electronics. The cumbersome v-seal in his hands made movement difficult, even with one-gee artificial gravity.

His ears popped from the decreasing pressure. His heart raced. Shifting into position, he braced between the tear in the hull and a rack of oxygen cylinders. Aligning the v-seal over the wound, he activated its magnetic latch, letting it slip into place. The artificial breezes faded as the patch held. Moments later the ship's alarms ceased. But the memories didn't.

Devin squeezed his eyes tight, trying to force the unwanted images from his mind. He slumped against the cylinder rack.

Cold metal valves jabbed against his back. He turned and inspected them, hoping for a reprieve from his thoughts.

Devin had salvaged the four cylinders a few weeks back, and like most items of potential use he retrieved, they'd been piled into the cargo hold. There, along with a score of other junk and debris, they waited, forgotten.

He noted the cylinders: Each was about one-half meter in diameter and two meters in length; while one end of the cylinder was rounded, the other end was fitted with a pressure release valve. One of cylinders was missing a valve.

"Everything okay back there? " Allison's smooth voice came over the ship's intercom. She was the newbie pilot Devin had hired before the launch a couple days ago.

He checked the remaining cylinders.

"Devin . . . ? Can you hear me? "

"Yeah. I'm all right," he answered. "Just getting my hearing back."

"What hit us? Our scanners show nothing in the area."

A chill crawled over Devin's body.

"Looks like one of the O^2 cylinders back here popped a release valve," he said." The damned thing musta blew right through the hull."

"Should we dump them before any more go? "An indefinable accent danced upon every other syllable of Allison's words.

Devin shook his head; she was a newbie and had plenty to learn.

"When you salvage for a living," he said, "you never throw away anything that you can use. And we can definitely use O^2."

He thought he heard her snicker. "We'll certainly need it if we keep losing it."

Devin checked the remaining cylinders, verifying they were snug in their cradles. He wondered about Allison. What was a navy-quality pilot doing on the fringe, working a salvage ship? *Running*, the answer came. And the fringe was the best place to hide. *In the salvage biz you pick up a lot of things*, Devin thought, *and sometimes it's best if you don't question where they came from*. Allison was a good pilot, and he had decided when he hired her not to pry.

"While you were back there, I narrowed down the location of our mysterious broadcast."

"Did it start transmitting again? " Devin asked anxiously.

"Yeah. And if everything's secure, I'll take us there."

"Don't waste any time. Heading fore right now."

* * *

The *Redeemer's* bridge was small and confining — just enough space for two people to move around, though not at once. While rebuilding the salvaged freighter ship, Devin hadn't worried about crew comforts. His principal concern had been available room for salvaged items — his lifeblood. In fact, only mandatory instrumentation and equipment had even made it aboard the heavily modified craft.

Allison was sitting in the pilot's chair, head cocked, almond eyes intently gazing at the passive scanner display above the viewport. Devin admired her hard beauty; her compact frame was taut and sculpted with lean edges; her brown hair sheared short.

"That it? " he asked, squeezing himself into the copilot's seat.

The forward floods washed light over a twisted and tangled heap of metal in front of the *Redeemer*. It remained motionless. Allison had matched its speed and course.

"I think so," she said." We were within one-thousand klicks when it started broadcasting again."

"Did you do an active scan? Maybe that started it? "

"Uh-uh. Didn't do anything."

"Strange," he whispered.

They'd been chasing the transmission since setting out. Its broadcasts were incoherent garbage, and they appeared to occur at random intervals. Being in such close proximity this last time seemed to be pure luck. "I think I'll take Murphy out and poke around."

Allison chewed on her lower lip, her eyes watching something far away. "Think it could be an alien ship? "

Excitement welled inside Devin. Usually every vulture in the sector had picked over the wrecks by the time he'd reached them. This time it looked like he first to arrive. And if it were the remains of an alien vessel, it would be worth a fortune.

Devin linked into the *Redeemer's* computer, plugging the ship's cable into microjack at the base of his skull. "We might have something here."

Allison nodded, still distant.

"Keep an eye out," he said. "I'll be blind for a few minutes."

"With this thing broadcasting," he continued, "everyone in the sector will be heading here. Let's make sure we get ours first, and get out, before the rest show."

"Gotcha," Allison said, reaching for an instrument cluster. She flicked several switches, and then abruptly turned to Devin. "Weapon system control doesn't respond . . . it's dead."

He smiled, trying to appear optimistic. "No weapons. When I found the ship they'd already been stripped, and I couldn't afford replacements. Besides, they take up too much space."

Confusion seemed to settle over Allison's hard countenance. But before she could protest, Devin activated the connection with the ship's computer.

✱ ✱ ✱

The remote probe, Murphy, drifted through night and stars toward the alien hulk. Its artificial limbs extended to full length, in case Devin misjudged the distance — the sharp edges of reality softened in virtual space, adding a dreamy quality to perception.

As Devin approached the craft, thousands of tiny digital spiders crawled across his face, arms and chest. The sensation, he knew, was created by the telepresence software's translation of Murphy's input sensors. High amplitude RF waves coming from the ruined ship produced the feeling. Nothing more than an electronic mirage, Devin thought. He glided in closer.

Most of the free-floating mass was damaged hull. The ship it had belonged to probably slammed into an asteroid. *Hopefully, there was enough left to salvage.* First, he needed to locate the source of the broadcast.

Devin activated Murphy's cutting laser.

Minutes crept by as the probe worked diligently, under Devin's remote command. After cutting a series of crossed lines in the alloy, he peeled open the sliced hull as though it were a gigantic piece of metallic fruit, using Murphy's claws.

The intensity of the alien broadcast increased when the insulating barrier opened. The tingle transformed into needles. Devin shuddered as electro-magnetic bursts slammed against his virtual body. He commanded Murphy to decrease input sensitivity, alleviating some of the pain.

Years of experience had given him the skill to move the mechanical arms with great precision. Gingerly he reached the probe's arm into the gap. With Murphy's limited tactile sensors he felt a hard, vibrating surface — the source of the transmission. *Got it.*

He commanded the probe to grip the object and gently pull. The thing refused to budge. If it were attached to something, cutting it free would be impossible. Again he tried. This time it snapped loose. Murphy's arm retracted, clutching the prize.

Through the remote's artificial eyes, Devin gazed at the treasure. It was an opaque green — at least to Murphy's optics — and ovoid in shape. An active scan revealed it possessed considerable mass. And after Devin had removed it, the broadcast halted. He waited, half expecting the thing to explode.

"Devin." Allison's voice filled his world. She'd linked the ship's intercom into the computer. "We have a problem."

Even though Devin was physically in the chair next to Allison, he couldn't speak while linked into the computer. The software he used to connect with Murphy lacked the routines to translate thoughts into speech. And while connected, his body remained partially paralyzed. Only the autonomic functions continued.

Still, the edge in Allison's voice told him all he needed to know. He scanned the surrounding starfield, expecting his fears to take shape. Through Murphy, Devin spied an approaching ship. Its mongrel form and mishmash collection of armor identified it better than any transponder beacon. He looked away, returning Murphy's eyes to the alien object.

"Company's coming, so you'd better get that thing quick," Allison said. "These guys don't sound friendly."

Maybe he could trick them. After all, the broadcast had stopped, just like so many times before. Or maybe he could bargain — memories flickered through his mind, he forced them away.

Devin guided the remote clear of the tangled metal heap, then started toward the *Redeemer.* After caching a series of commands to Murphy, he disconnected.

* * *

"Talk, *Junkman*, or we gonna get ma-had," a voice whined over the ship's comm.

Seconds passed while Devin adjusted to his new reality. "Have they said anything else? " he managed.

"Nothing worth repeating."

"Have you spoken to them yet? "

She shook her head. "No. They seemed to know you, so I thought I'd let you handle it." Her eyes drifted toward the defunct weapons panel.

Devin leaned forward, pressing the transmit button on the console. "This salvage is claimed," he said. "You have no . . ."

"Wrong answer, *Junkman*," the voice interrupted. "Didn't know you had rights to this wreck. Hope you not gonna tell the sector captain on us? " Raucous laughter punctuated the transmission.

Devin slumped back, raking his hair with both hands. Out of the corner of his eye he glimpsed Allison, her form pressed into the chair, arms laced, lips tight, eyes wide. Then he remembered the *others*. Something dark inside him shifted.

"Who are they? " she asked.

The question surprised him. Then he realized what she'd meant. "Scabs . . .," he said hesitantly. "Pirates."

"How many are there on the ship? " Allison asked.

"More than we can deal with."

"Great," she tossed up her hands. "In that case, why don't you tell me what you found *before* we hand it over."

"I don't know," he said. "Looks like an egg. Just a hell of a lot heavier."

"Alien? " Allison suggested.

The possibility seemed good. Either that or military.

"*Junkman*," the singsong voice came. "We know why you're so quiet. Hiding something. Keepin' safe that newbie flyer you got."

Allison's dark eyes narrowed. "How . . .? " she started.

"News travels fast on the fringe worlds," Devin said. "Especially if anyone thinks there's a price on your head."

Allison turned a stony gaze to the viewport.

"Tell you the deal, *Junkman*. Give us the newbie, and you keep the salvage." A chorus of cheers erupted at the suggestion.

"Solid with you? "

Suddenly Devin understood. The scabs didn't know he had the alien device, maybe didn't know about it at all. They'd tracked him down with other intentions.

"What do you figure it's worth? " Allison asked.

He didn't answer. Fear crept through his body, slowly taking root.

"Come on!" the speaker blared, distorted. "You traded us wreck survivors before. What makes a newbie so special? "

Before the scab had finished, Allison jumped to her feet facing Devin. Revulsion and anger twisted her face.

"What's it worth? " she demanded, her posture rigid, muscles like tense springs, waiting to release.

He inhaled. "I had to do it . . . ," he said, talking more to himself than her. "I had no choice. They were survivors; I'd have lost the salvage."

Allison's eyes went wide.

"Things are different out here," Devin went on, raising a hand to silence her. "You have to look out for yourself."

"How much is that damned thing worth? " she screamed.

He paused. His heart pounded in his chest, its sheer force threatening to break his ribs. "I don't know —" he moved his shoulders — "a lot."

Her gaze burned. They both knew what he'd really said was, "*It's worth more than you.*"

Allison stepped to the center of the small bridge. Her movement stiff, her hands clasped into tight fists. In a subdued tone she said, "You keep it . . . I'll go over."

At her words, something cold and dark inside Devin cracked, shattering into a million pieces. He knew what she expected of him, what the scabs expected of him, even what he expected of himself. Bile rose in his throat.

"No," he whispered. "No."

"I can look out for myself." Her eyes became dark pools void of emotion.

"No. They're slavers. It makes no difference–"

Thuum! The *Redeemer* shuddered. The growl of metal grating against metal filled the ship. Decompression alarms sounded.

Devin spun around, checking the console. A score of indicators and images flickered across the displays. A missile had impacted on the *Redeemer's* midsection.

The comm crackled, mixing with the howl of alarms. "Just waking you up, *Junkman*. Thought maybe you fell asleep."

"Get into your en-suit," he said, climbing from his seat. "We have to decompress . . ."

Devin halted. Allison no longer stood before him. But what stood there was not human. The only similarities it possessed were basic shapes: head, torso, arms, legs, all bloated and void of detail, as though it were nothing more than a grotesque, misshapen human sculpture that had been placed on display in the center of *Redeemer's* bridge. He dropped against the console.

"It's me," the featureless mass croaked. "Allison."

Memories raced through Devin's mind. He'd heard of an alien race that had such exacting control over their muscles that they were capable of altering their own physical appearance. He'd never encountered one — that he knew of.

"I am a Krorian," it said. "I will go aboard the pirate vessel as Allison. Once they dock, I will alter myself. They will never find me."

"No," he said flatly, surprising himself with the finality of his tone. "If you go over there, they'll place you in coldsleep until they can trade you or sell you. You won't have a chance."

"There is no other option. If you do not comply, they will destroy both of us and the ship."

Devin spun and slapped the alarm button. Silence poured over them. "I'm not doing it again," he said. "I can't. But I'm going to need your help."

The Krorian's face was round and shapeless and uncaring, like the surface of a distant, icy moon. It remained silent.

"We don't have much time," Devin pressed.

After a long moment, the alien asked: "What do you need me to do? "

A thin smile formed on Devin's lips. "Just keep them busy while I try something." He dropped into the copilot's seat and linked into the *Redeemer's* computer.

* * *

The darkness of space embraced Devin, filling his mind with an endless field of stars. He was drifting alongside the *Redeemer*, still clutching the alien device.

Using the remotes maximum thrust, he navigated around the ship, toward the exterior cargo bay hatch.

"Attenuate Murphy's sensor levels." It was Allison's voice, the smooth one he'd remembered. At least that explains the accent, he thought.

Devin reduced the remote's sensitivity; he'd done so before when retrieving the alien device, but not knowing what Allison had in mind, he thought it best to do it again. His vision dimmed, making the black void around him vague and indistinct. Numbness filled his body.

"Their missiles use an RF tracking system," Allison said, "real rusting-edge stuff. On the next launch I'm going to configure our active scanners to transmit a broad spectrum signal. That should confuse the targeting system." She added, "I'd like to try some evasive maneuvers, but this ship is too slow for anything like that."

If that doesn't work, Devin thought, *we can always throw rocks.*

He approached the hold door and signaled the ship's to decompress the hold and cut its artificial gravity — Murphy could only maneuver under zero-gee or micro-gee environment. Next Devin commanded the hold doors open.

As the remote entered the cargo hold, he heard Allison. "They've launched . . . Here goes our countermeasures."

Searing pain burned inside Devin's head; acid filled every space between his muscles. Long, awful seconds passed before the burning ended.

"It worked," she said with a hint of satisfaction. "Now if I only had something to fire back at them."

Although his body still ached, he directed the probe inside the ship. He hoped to finish before the scabs sent another missile.

Devin knew the *Redeemer's* cargo hold well enough to navigate through it blind, but that was with gravity. Now that everything inside the hold was in free-fall, he could only guess at a path. Gingerly, he navigated over and around the drifting debris — door motors, array antennas, damaged coldsleep modules, storage lockers, tools and myriad other items, all salvaged material he'd intended to sort out some day. He glided through the random clutter until locating the O^2 cylinder rack. With a command, he released the alien egg, hoping it wasn't magnetically glued to Murphy's claws, the same way a piece of sticky paper clung to flesh.

The thing danced into the darkness. Clamping Murphy's claws onto the rack, Devin filtered back through the maze of junk until he exited the hold.

In the silence of space, the remote drifted alongside the ship. Hopefully the scab radar lacked the sensitivity to distinguish Murphy and the rack from the *Redeemer*. His scheme required surprise, and he'd only get one chance. Soon the scabs would grow tired of their play and either board or destroy the ship. Under Devin's guidance, Murphy hauled the O^2 rack into position above the *Redeemer*. After aiming the rounded ends of the cylinders toward the scab craft, he maneuvered Murphy clear of the release valves — he'd already seen the damage they were capable of doing.

Allison's voice returned. "They just offered us our last chance."

The scab ship appeared vague and distant through Murphy's sensors. To improve his chances, Devin jacked up the input levels. A sharp pain danced along his nerves; his vision cleared, contrasting the scab ship against the background.

With his nerves on fire, he angled the cylinders directly at the scab ship. Keeping one of Murphy's claws on the rack to stabilize it, he used the other to snap free the first release valve.

Four thousand pounds per square inch of pure oxygen rushed through the valve's narrow opening. The cylinder rocketed from its cradle, a comet of metal streaming through space.

Almost immediately Devin felt the stinging of a narrow-focus jamming signal — electronic countermeasures. However, the primitive torpedo had no guidance to be confused. It soared onward, slamming into its target.

The ship's tattered armor plating buckled inward on impact. Atmosphere gushed into space, forming a cloud of shimmering crystals.

Suddenly, the *Redeemer* fired its thrusters, gaining velocity, wheeling away from Murphy. The action surprised Devin. Then he noticed the orange glow of a chemical rocket streaking toward the *Redeemer*. The searing pain returned. Only this time it felt as though he'd been dropped on the surface of a star. Millions of white-hot needles pierced his skin. But, as abruptly as the agony had started, it vanished. His vision blurred. It felt like he were spinning. Through the haze he sensed a missile burning past the *Redeemer*.

"The ECM transmitter just crisped," Allison said. "The next missile hits."

Devin struggled to clear the pain from his mind. Murphy was no longer hiding in the *Redeemer's* electronic shadow, and it wouldn't take long to figure out where the makeshift torpedoes were coming from.

Once again he adjusted the O^2 rack, using Murphy's active scan to focus on the target. In quick succession, he snapped the remaining release valves. The burst of escaping oxygen propelled the cylinders across the distance, one trailing the other. Streaks of ice traced their path. Devin watched.

The jamming signal's sting returned, though it no longer bothered Devin.

The torpedoes continued.

Orange blooms erupted from the scab ship's thrusters, maneuvering to avoid impact. Its velocity increased rapidly.

Cold despair swelled inside Devin's chest as he realized that both missiles would miss their target. All that was left now was the *Redeemer*. The words of an Old Earth philosopher shimmered unbidden in his mind: "*It's better to burn out, then fade away . . ..*" He severed the link with Murphy.

Eons passed by as Devin focused his consciousness. He was back in the *Redeemer's* noisy bridge. Several minor alarms chimed." Good shootin'," Allison said.

Eyes closed, Devin lolled his head against the thin cushion of his chair. Formless shadows played across the inside of his eyelids. Switching between realities was beginning to take its toll. "Not good enough," he managed weakly.

"It was good enough for them."

Forcing his eyes open, Devin gazed through the viewport.

The scab ship continued its acceleration. Only the yellow blossom of its engines remained visible as it headed into the abyss of space.

Nice to see someone else run for once, Devin thought.

Three weeks in dock at *Glaive* station had passed while the *Redeemer* underwent repairs. Devin had collected a firm quarter-mil in credits for the alien device, which turned out to be a transponder. But as soon as they'd hit dock, Allison vanished with her share.

The ship refits would take at least four weeks, so Devin hadn't bothered looking for another pilot. He wasn't even sure he wanted one.

During his stay at the station, he'd thought about going out, maybe visiting a few casinos or bars or worse. He'd never really had the credits for nightlife and entertainment before. He'd never really wanted to experience them. Too many people.

Instead he stayed on the ship, pushing the modifications ahead, checking on the work, and joining in when needed. He filled his days working, and nights prowling the ship's crawlways checking cabling and upgrading junctions. At those times the ship was empty and still.

He'd been in the crawlway beneath the cargo hold when his routine changed. Footsteps clanged across the deck above him. Like all news on the fringe, Devin knew word of his find had spread — and maybe rumors of his past. He crouched beneath the deck, squeezing a wrench.

The footsteps halted. He wondered if the scabs had come to *Glaive* station to repay him. He remained still. *A wrench is useless*, he thought. *But so is an O² cylinder*. As he hunkered in the crawlway he listened to the pings and clicks echoing throughout the ship. He'd always cut and run from his problems in the past. Doing so had made him weary. Instead, he decided to take the offensive. Quietly, he moved toward the ladder.

"I didn't think this ship could look this clean," a familiar voice said.

Devin poked his head through the hatch in the floor. Allison stood before him, her face as he'd remembered it. "I didn't expect to see you again — at least this version of you," he said.

"I was thinking the same thing about you," she replied. "Sorry about disappearing. I had some business to finish. My popularity has decreased, you might say."

"I think I understand," Devin said. Being a bit of a shape-shifter himself, he knew the troubles that went with it. "I'd hoped to celebrate our discovery . . . and victory." He arched an eyebrow. "I'll buy."

Allison laughed. The sound filled the empty cargo hold." You'll have to, 'cause I've spent all my credits on weapons."

"Planning to go to war? "

"No. But I've got another year on my contract, and I'm not going out on this ship unarmed."

Devin nodded, then climbed onto the deck.

"I think I'm out of the salvage business," he said. "Don't know what I'll do. But you're welcome to stay on."

Allison strolled through along the deck, cocking her head from side-to-side. "It's a good ship. Maybe we can salvage something besides junk."

The words echoed against the ship's metal skin. Slowly, Devin paced the hold's length, remembering the clutter that had once filled every space. There was much to reclaim, he thought. And most if it wasn't junk.

ARTIFACTS   87

TALES OF A
CURIOUS PAST

RAWHIDE AND BLOODYBONES

WHEN YOU GET OLD enough, just about every day is an anniversary, if you have a head for it. Here, at the Shady Hills retirement home, our little club of seniors enjoys sharing anniversaries. In fact, we have so many combined years among us that sometimes these special days overlap.

We gather everyday in the community room and chat and spin yarns and listen. I normally don't partake in this little entertainment because I don't have much of a head for such things. There are, in fact, few days in my ninety-one years that I can single out as memorable. And I suppose those few which should be, aren't because I forgot to remember them at the time. So, I typically sit beyond the circle of gatherers and eavesdrop. That, however, was about to change.

Now, Sara Young has an anniversary just about every confound day of the year. She's eighty-six and believes not a day has slipped from her head. She claims to remember her first day of grade-school, the first time she rode a bicycle — alone and unaided — , her first date — which was with her husband Howard —, her first kiss — also Howard's handiwork — , the first time she watched a television — yes, there are a few of us who remember when there was no such thing as a rerun — , and she even says she can remember the first time she tasted *Coca-Cola*. But what strikes me odd about Sara and her bear trap of a memory is that she cannot remember Howard is dead. When she's not going-on about some anniversary, she's standing alone at the gates of Shady Hills, waiting for him to drive up. No one here has the heart to tell her otherwise.

Being a warm spring day, I had fully expected to be listening to one of Sara's dry and dusty tales about the first time she had received flowers or some such thing. But that didn't happen. For some reason Sara was in a listening mood. The floor was open.

It is the custom of our little group to ask each member if they have an anniversary. Excluding Sara's unexpected silence, things were going as usual. As the question made its way around the room, I noticed a sparkle in Charlie Hopkins' eyes; and as each person declined that sparkle grew brighter.

Charlie always kept a war story at the ready. During World War II he had done a four-year stint in Europe, and he was always looking for a means of reminding us. I didn't mind Charlie's stories much, though they are a bit repetitious. At least there is more action in them than Sara's.

The question continued around the community room without anything turning up. This brought Charlie to the bursting point. From the radiant look in his eyes, I could tell he thought he had won the day. However, the question would be put to me before Charlie — the group wanted to turn over every stone before resorting to one of Charlie Hopkins' windy war stories. I hated sneaking up on him that way, but he was five years younger than I, and he would always have another chance tomorrow, a confidence I lacked.

Vera Brown runs the show in the community room, and pretty much everywhere else at the Hills. She puts the question to each person and has final say on it being a proper anniversary or not. Vera and I go together like a match and a can of gasoline. I think she is cantankerous and snooty, though those words fall short of the mark, and she dislikes the way I dress, mainly my style of clothes and color. I don't know who elected her president of our little club; all I know is that the next time elections come around I intend to vote. Many times I've tried to convey that I don't much care how I dress, so long as I have enough cloth to cover my sack of bones, but she never listens. I expected a sharp word from her, but it would be worth the price. Finally, Vera brought the question to me.

"Lloyd, do you have a story?" she asked, clearly not expecting anything. Gravel and grit rolled around in her throat, at least that's how her voice sounded to me, and always has for the three years I've had the honor and privilege of her acquaintance. I know my voice has a few wrinkles where it once had been smooth, but for some reason I figure hers has always sounded about the same. A truck driving over an old gravel road.

Few eyes set on me when Vera asked the question. Probably no one had expected me to have anything to say, so they wasted no energy looking my way. Conservation of such resources becomes a priority when you reach the average age at Shady Hills.

I cleared my throat and answered. "Yes. Today is an anniversary for me."

Wide-eyed stares, exaggerated expressions and the squeal of hearing aids filled the somber community room. Even Charlie's eyes fixed on me, their scintillation turned into something more akin to the dull glow of a smoldering fire.

"It's about time, Lloyd," Emma called out. "I've wondered when you were going to join in and give us a story. I figured you'd get over your shyness after a while."

Emma is the youngest member of our senior's club, eighty-three, and the newest resident to Shady Hills. She is also the sassiest old woman I have ever known.

"Yes . . . get over here and tell us," others joined. I doubt that my unexpected offering honestly intrigued anyone. On the contrary, I believe no one wanted to hear Charlie's story, so they enthusiastically ushered me over to the sitting-circle.

I shuffled across the room. I don't use a cane, though I probably should, I suppose I'm just stubborn in that way. Sometimes it takes me a while to get where I'm going, but I eventually get there.

"Good heavens, Lloyd! Those brown pants *do not* match that shirt!" I was obviously in range of Vera's style-sensitive eyes.

"Too bad," I retorted, my own eyes glued to my feet and the floor beneath them. "I guess I won't win the fashion show today."

"Oh leave the poor man alone, Vera," Emma piped in. "Who's going to care how he's dressed any how?"

"I care," Vera said indignantly. "I live in a retirement home, not a circus."

I settled down into one of the chairs, letting its soft cushions break my fall. "Deal with it, Vera," I said after catching my breath. "I like the way I dress." Then I mustered up my smuggest grin and added, "I'm trendy."

Though I can't say for certain, I believe Vera's eyes rolled. When your vision starts to go, you learn to read body actions, and most of the members of the senior's club quickly learned to make grand gestures to accompany the subtler ones or to limit the gestures for only those intended.

"So what is this anniversary?" Charlie asked truculently. I realized his last hope was that I had a short story.

"I don't have much of a head for remembering things the way most of you do, but sometimes a memory pops into my mind, though seldom on the proper day," I started my prologue. "However, there are certain things I do remember. The day my mother died. The day my father died. The day I came here. And today."

"Only the good things, huh?" Charlie chuckled.

"Well then, what's today?" Vera asked.

I forced a smile on my face. I was nervous and out of practice. "Sixty-six years ago, to this day." I leaned forward and peeked out the wide frame of windows hanging in one wall. High in the eastern sky the sun burned. I figured it to be around ten o'clock. "Just about this time sixty-six years ago, give or take a few minutes — "I could tell that my precision annoyed Vera, which delighted me — "I killed a man."

The room was silent.

In 1934, I was twenty-three, a high-school English teacher, and smack-dab in the middle of the Great Depression. I had been born and raised in Chicago, so when I graduated from the University of Illinois, I wanted to teach in Chicago. Times were hard then and jobs scarce; after eleven months of grinding out a living selling used cars, I decided to say farewell to the city. Without my hope of teaching in Chicago, there was nothing to anchor me there.

My parents had passed on before I had graduated from college; my mother first in 1918 from Influenza. Then my father in '23, from what may be considered natural causes in Chicago. His small south central bookstore was robbed, and he was murdered for the price of a few Dime Novels.

So, with my parents and hope of teaching in the city lost, I headed south. Two months later I found myself planted in the mountains of North Carolina. There, in a small town named Jefferson, I landed a teaching job at the only high school around, Jefferson High. I found that little town to be surprisingly hospitable to Yankee English teachers.

Jefferson High was my first honest teaching job. And you might expect me to remember most of my first pupils — I know a few teachers who can. But for the life of me, I can't. In fact, of the forty years I taught, I can only remember a handful of students. Ten years ago the number ranged around a baker's dozen, but time has eroded and softened the edges of my mind.

I've been told that memory is the first to go, but I know that isn't true. And in my case, memory didn't go fast enough. No, no, there is a whole catalog of things that go before memory: Vision, teeth, legs, friends, loved-ones and conscience. Though for most people it isn't in that order. With some folks, conscience is the first, and then the others follow in a line. I know . . . I lost mine on May 26th of '34.

But well before that, I was on my way to losing my vision. I guess this was to be expected. Many a-doctor had warned me against reading books, saying the habit would make me myopic. A small price the way I figured things. Yet, by May of '34, the dunning for my pleasure had commenced.

I first noticed it during morning attendance. The world beyond my desk had become a blurry mess, and squinting was the only thing that would bring it back into focus. I had to squint to make out the faces of my students. This often solicited a similar response from the more gregarious of my pupils — though I never let on that I noticed. But on the morning of May 25th, this affliction led me to calling a student's name twice. Rachel Hampton. She was one of those students who silently responded by raising her hand. I had been expecting her to be present that Friday; but she wasn't.

The world is filled with bright students, plenty enough for every teacher. Rachel was my first and finest and most memorable. When I asked a question, her arm was the quickest, straightest and longest. Sometimes I feared she would knock her gangly body right out of the chair the way her arm rocketed skyward.

The reason I had expected Rachel to turn up in class on this particular day was the topic: *Sir Orfeo*. She had fiery red hair, large almond eyes and a burning, romantic heart. I know the time for romanticism is long past. Today Manfred's pleadings for self-oblivion would garner him a quick prescription for *Prozac*, and a dream on St. Agnes' Eve would result in a trip to an analyst. No, this is not the century of romanticism, it is the century of cynicism, and there is no room for the likes of Byron and Keats in it.

Even so, I still taught the romantics and romance literature. And these works were some of Rachel's favorites. True, *Sir Orfeo* was a medieval retelling of the ancient *Orpheus in the Underworld* — and it was put to vellum long before the romantic period, but nonetheless it was a chivalric romance, and one guaranteed to keep Rachel on the edge of her seat. Besides, I've always believed that a tale worth telling once is worth retelling in a different fashion, again and again. So, on that Friday, I was prepared to read *Sir Orfeo* to the class, from my own copy — Jefferson had a limited budget for books and supplies — and Rachel was not present.

When I had called her name that morning I had expected her to be there, so I automatically went on to the next name before realizing I hadn't seen her. I raised my head and scanned the room, squinting to bring the faces into focus. She was not there. This was her fourth consecutive absence. A record for her.

Sometimes students simply drop out of school, even the Rachel Hamptons. There are always bountiful reasons for this, and in '34 the list seemed endless. Though I had only been at Jefferson for ten months, I had seen many students stop attending. In a rural farming community, and during the Depression, help was always needed at home. Students were easily lost. And while losing any student is hard, sometimes losing a Rachel Hampton was that much harder.

After Rachel's second absence, I had devised a plan. I announced that on Friday I would be reading *Sir Orfeo*. I had anticipated that such news would arrive on Rachel's doorstep in some fashion. After all, Jefferson was a small town and news, dreadful or pleasant, eventually found its way to every student. Yet, Rachel was absent. I continued the attendance and conducted class to a mostly bleary eyed audience.

Sir Orfeo is a tale of queens, kings, knights, honor, romance and duty. In this thoroughly romantic story, Orfeo's bride is kidnapped and carried away to a fairyland were she finds herself the prisoner of a grim king. Orfeo's duty is clear. A task he accepts without an inkling of self-concern, guided by his perfect chivalric love for his wife and queen. Today we'd say that Orfeo possessed a genetically pre-programmed strategy that promoted self-sacrifice for the good of his species, or that he was sexually obsessed, but when the tale was written, Orfeo was in love. Nothing more. Nothing less. Lust didn't fire Orfeo onward. Pure, noble love did.

By the last class of that day, I had decided I had a duty too. Since telephones were a rare luxury in those days, I decided to pay a visit to the Hampton house. I intended to bring her any missed class work and leave my copy of *Sir Orfeo*, in case its magic was needed.

What most people in Jefferson called hills I called mountains. Any lump in the ground higher than a house is a mountain to me. Jefferson was set in the middle of hills and mountains, making the roads full of twists and turns and turns and twists. Here and there a secondary road, usually a dirt road, sprouted from the main highway, these were the roads that led to the houses; however, the main road folded and wrapped and snaked around mountains of slate and shale and grass, making driving hazardous, at least for an automobile. Fortunately my Cabriolet topped out at twenty-five miles an hour, so I was never at too great a risk unless I closed my eyes.

After a brief, though dizzying journey, I turned off the highway onto the gravel road that snaked up a hill to the Hampton house. There I parked and climbed the broad wooden steps of the porch and knocked on the screen door.

Soon a dark-haired woman, an aged and weary version of Rachel, appeared at the door.

"Hello, Mrs. Hampton," I said. "I'm Lloyd Weaver, ma'am.

Rachel's teacher at Jefferson."

"Oh howdy!" she called back more enthusiastically than her slight body seemed capable, and the screen door swung open. "Won't you please come in?"

We entered the living room. A frayed cloth couch, a similar high-back chair, a threadbare rocking chair with scarred arms, and a broad fireplace inhabited the large room. Flowery paper clung to the walls transforming the room into a field of daffodils.

"Please make yourself comfortable, Mr. Weaver," said Mrs. Hampton.

My apology and explanation for my unannounced visit caught in my throat when a girl dashed into the room. A purple and white striped dress, similar in fashion to a dress Rachel often wore, dangled on the girl. She bore a resemblance to Rachel while differing in an equal degree. I guessed her to be a year or two beyond Rachel, eighteen or nineteen perhaps.

"This is my daughter, Mary. Mary, this is Mr. Weaver, Rachel's high school teacher."

"Hello Mary. Please," I said to both, "call me Lloyd. I'm only Mr. Weaver in a school house."

"Mary, go fetch Mr. Weaver some lemonade out of the spring-house. He must be burnin' up after his ride."

Mary rushed off.

Even then I admired the zest and energy of youth, always in a hurry to reach a destination and always in a hurry to return.

"I apologize for the unannounced visit, Mrs. Hampton. But I was concerned about Rachel. She hasn't been in school for nearly a week."

Mrs. Hampton mulled over my words in silence. Deep lines traced around her face.

"The poor thing isn't well at all, Mr. Weaver," she said after a moment. "Doctor Clayton says her body's just fine, that it's her mind . . . ."

The revelation stunned me. I started toward her but caught myself. "What has happened?" I asked.

"I don't rightfully know, Mr. Weaver. We just found her the other day a-wandering out in the fields. She was staring off in the distance as though she were seeing something . . . 'cept there weren't nothing there. We called for doctor Clayton, and he rushed right over. He said he ain't seen something like this in going-on thirty years. He calls it hysteria. Says she's just locked herself up in her mind and won't come out till she's good and ready."

I found myself grasping for something to say, but I found nothing. All of the words I had to offer felt too pale and too shallow.

"Do you think I could see her?"

"Certainly. She talks of you all the time. I reckon you must be her favorite teacher. Maybe seein' your face will wake her up."

We climbed the stairs to the second floor. At the top, Rachel's mother stopped. "Rachel, honey," she said. "Mr. Weaver, your teacher, is here to visit." Gently she pushed open the door.

Sitting on the bed, hunched against the headboard, was the young girl that had always been filled with energy and life. Her liquid eyes seemed to be searching some distant, dark land; her narrow arms lay limp at her side.

"Rachel," I said, approaching the bed. "Do you know who I am?"

No response.

I carried a yellow maple chair from across the room and placed it next to the bed.

"Has she said anything since you found her?" I asked Mrs. Hampton who was standing in the doorway, arms folded around herself. In her glassy eyes I could see the depth of her pain.

"No," she said, struggling with the word. "She ain't said a thing for nearly seven days now."

"Did the doctor say how long she would be like this?"

Rachel's mother stared beyond me as though she too was looking at some dark world of her own. "He doesn't know," she finally answered.

I understood her pain. I had known such desperation before, and I've known it since. Cruelly cut into that woman's visage was the same agony I had seen on my father's face when my mother lay in bed, wet with the sweat of Influenza. That ugly expression had been chiseled by his inability to do anything to help his dying wife. It is a mournful expression I will never forget.

"He asked advice of every man, but help King Orfeo, no

man can," I muttered softly.

"Mama!" A voice cried from downstairs. "That negra is comin' up to the house!"

"Excuse me," Rachel's mother said. The moment allowed her to regain composure. She marched down the stairs, calling to the livelier of her two daughters. "Good Lord, Mary. You'd think the world was a coming to an end the way you're hollarin'. There ain't nothing special about that man, he just don't have a home, that's it."

My eyes returned to Rachel. I didn't much believe in the doctor's diagnosis, and I wondered how much faith he stocked in it. Sometimes fear of someone or something can alter a man's perception. In a small town like Jefferson, pointing fingers wasn't always a good practice.

"What happened?" I asked softly. In silence she continued to stare at something only she could see.

Beyond the room I heard a hard and hurried clacking of feet on stairs, the sound of someone running. With a final flurry of pounding Mary arrived at the doorway.

"Mama told me to fetch you for dinner, Mr. Weaver," she said, puffing.

My first inclination was to refuse the hospitality. But with a second consideration, I decided to accept, hoping I might glean something more about Rachel's condition.

At the dinner table there were four of us: Mrs. Hampton, Mary, Milk Gamble — the black man who had caused such a commotion in Mary — and myself. While seeing a black man was not an event in my life, it apparently was for Mary. In Jefferson there were not many black men or women, the small town was predominately white.

"Mary, quit eyeing Mr. Gamble," Mrs. Hampton scolded.

"I'm sorry, mama. I just ain't never seen a negra this close before."

"Quit saying *ain't*," Mrs. Hampton continued her scolding, but this time with a quick glance my way.

"I than'ya much ma'm," said Milk Gamble. "I don' 'spect ya ta take me in an' feed me. I wuz jus' hopin' ya mightin' gives me a small sack a scrapes. Das all."

"Why Milk Gamble, my dead mother would tan my hide,

horse whip, tar and feather me if I didn't feed a person who was hungry. She always said 'feed a hungry man, it could be your own someday.'"

"I thanks'ya 'gain, ma'm."

As the meal progressed, I looked for an opening to continue my questioning. I didn't want to cast gloom over the meal, but I needed to understand.

"Who found Rachel?" I finally asked.

Rachel's mother had been tending more to the needs of her guests than her own. I suspected her daughter had not wandered far from her mind.

"My husband did," she said. "He's away now; he's a foreman for the road demolitioner, but last Friday noon he was out workin' in the top field when he spotted her. She was just wandering aimlessly. He carried her back here to the house."

"How does she eat? Does she feed herself?"

"No. I feed her. She chews but I don't reckon she tastes a thing."

"She ain't gon' an' a seen ol' Rawhide en Bloodybones is she?" Milk Gamble asked around a mouthful of food.

Mary snickered. Her mother shot a stern glance the girl's way.

"No, I don't think so, Mr. Gamble," Mrs. Hampton replied.

"Dey does dat ta a youn'in. Fright's 'em righ' up. Make's 'em jus' gaze at nothin'."

Wide-eyed and nearly laughing, Mary finally spoke. "Why that's just an old tale. Everyone knows that ain't . . . isn't true." She turned and smiled at me.

"Naw . . .," Milk Gamble furiously shook his head. "Folks b'lieve ets jussa tale. Dat's what folks b'lieve w'en dey don' 'member why sumphin is. But ets naw a tale. Naw at all. Why I 'member w'en I wuz 'round yo' age an' old John Dollah saw Rawhide en Bloodybones ober at de Devil's Stairs. He jussa stop talkin' an' a walkin' an' a eat'n'. He died 'bout two weeks after dat, jus' as quick as ya like."

Mrs. Hampton's fork clacked on her plate, she pushed herself from the table and walked into the kitchen without saying a word.

Milk Gamble called after her. "Why I'm sorry ta upset ya, ma'm. I didn' means ta. I wuz jus' talkin'. Don' ya mind a word I says."

The meal was finished in silence, and then we said our good-byes. Mrs. Hampton thanked me for coming all the way out there to see Rachel, and she thanked me for leaving my copy of *Sir Orfeo*. She said it would delight Rachel when she got better. Then she filled Milk Gamble's arms with a potato sack of food and told him never to be afraid to stop by again.

With a purple and red evening sky turning black I decided to get a move on. My eyes were of less use at night, and the mountain roads did nothing to help my vision.

Milk Gamble was on his way down the hill in front of the Hampton house when I decided to see if he would like a ride. I knew I would enjoy his company and thought it might prevent me from getting lost. Yet, even with these thoughts lining my head, I knew the real reason for my asking him. I wanted to learn more about Rawhide and Bloodybones. Like Milk, I believed there were more than just words behind most tales.

At first, Milk appeared leery of the invitation.

"I ain't nevah been on de insides of one of dem things and I's likely ta ol ta star'," he said.

"You'll enjoy it," I replied.

"Prob'ly, mista Weaver. But I don' wants ta get use' ta it."

His argument made all the sense in the world to me, but I convinced him just the same. I suspect, in the end, Milk Gamble's curiosity had gotten the best of him.

I started the engine and the Cabriolet chugged to the black-top. Once I felt secure on the highway, I asked, "How does a person go about finding Rawhide and Bloodybones?"

A deep, soft laugh escaped Milk Gamble. I have heard the sound before, at college. It was the sound certain kindly profes-sors made when students asked naïve questions.

"I don' reckon ya kin find 'em. Least if ya lookin' fer 'em. Dey finds ya," he said above the rumble and clank of the engine.

"Then who or what are they?" I asked. The headlights of the car were faint on the blacktop. The surrounding mountains and trees seemed to swallow the dim light they cast.

"Dey's evil," he spit words like a man might spit out venom.

"Dey's no good. Dey's what makes men bad. Some men, if dey git a wiff of ol' Rawhide en Bloodybones, dey's 'come jus like 'em. Mean an' ugly. Dey'll kill an' steal an' be plain righ' evil. Dey take ta it like a fish takes ta water or a bird ta air or a snake ta de groun'. But udder folks . . ."

Out of the corner of my eye I saw Milk Gamble look at me. His eyes glistened in the faint light. He used them to do more than look. He was summing me up. With that single glance, I believe Milk Gamble knew as much about me as any person has ever known. His eyes were capable of looking inside and seeing what was hidden within.

"Udder folks," he continued, "dey don' mix well wi' ol' Rawhide en Bloodybones. Dey's good folks. Dey's the kin' Rawhide en Bloodybones like ta git a hol' of. Why ol' Rawhide en Bloodybones, dey wan's ta make doze folks bad like de udders. Dey wants dem ta star' a killin' an' stealin' an' lyin'. Mos' a'times dey do. But sometimes dey don'. Sometimes dey jussa catches a glimpse of Rawhide en Bloodybones an' dey go away from dis here worl'. Ets jus' too much fer 'em. Like dat li'le gal up yonda', she's done gone an glanc' at 'em en she's a hidin'. Jus' like de Bible says: A man can't see all of Gawd in one good look. An' a man can' see ol' Rawhide en Bloodybones in one gander, eitha. Least a good man can't. But even a li'le peek will stain 'em fer life. Et will pull at 'em an' fight wi' 'em an' try ta make 'em rotten. An' if'n dey don' give in ta dat rottenness, den dey sometimes locks demselves up where no one can gits ta 'em."

The road kept slipping from the dull beams of the headlights. I did my best to hold the car to one side of the road and listen to Milk Gamble. But apparently one or the other of my attentions was beginning to make Milk nervous; his eyes moved from me to the road in front.

"How do you get rid of these two unearthly fellows?" I asked after a few moments of struggling with the steering wheel. In those days automobiles did not have power steering, so the faster you drove the easier it was to control the car. Now I understand this falls under the laws of physics, but there was always something unsettling about it to me.

"You can't," Milk Gamble answered.

"Then how do you save a young girl from the clutches of

these demons?" I pressed.

"You pra', I s'pose." His voice was somber but the words seemed to drift in the car for long moments. "Here —" he pointed a narrow finger out his side window —"here is were dey say ol' Rawhide en Bloodybones rests. Mos' folks keeps clea' of dat place."

Without thinking, my foot jammed hard against the brake-pedal. Though the Cabriolet could not have been traveling more than twenty-five miles an hour, it squealed and swayed on the blacktop. Long seconds passed before the automobile slid to a stop. A few yards behind lay the dirt road Milk Gamble had indicated.

His creased face was full of excitement; his jaw hung low, revealing the toothless darkness within. I briefly worried that my action had caused his heart to fail, if not, at least a skip a beat. The expression on Milk Gamble's face told me this was not only his first automobile ride, but his last as well.

"Are you okay?" I asked.

He took a moment to ponder my question, then answered. "I've hear' rabbits scream like dat w'en dey's been caugh' in a snare, but I ain't nevah hear' a machine cry like dat."

I smiled. "Nothing to be concerned about. That's just my driving. The automobile didn't want to stop when I wanted to."

The old man nodded understandingly. "Ya fixin' ta go hunt-up ol' Rawhide en Bloodybones ain't ya?"

"I have to help that girl," I said.

"Ya may hurt yerself a tryin'."

"That's okay. I've learned that there is a price for every-thing."

"Dat be da troof," he said. "Dat be de Lawd's troof."

He examined the door in the dim moonlight, his frail fingers moving over the interior. "Is dey a knob or sumphin ta grab on ta'?" he asked.

"Yes." I reached over and pulled the handle, the door popped open.

Milk Gamble climbed from the Cabriolet, turned, pulled out his sack, pushed the door closed, and then peered into the automobile. "I'd come an' he'p ya if I could; but I fear I'd do ya mo' ha'm dan good." He loaded a heavy, toothless grin onto his face. "I ain't as youn' as I's used ta be . . . .."

"It isn't your job," I said.

"Oh, it is. It surely is. I jus' can' do it anymo'. I'm too ol' an' creaky."

I started the engine — it had stalled in the excitement. "You've all ready helped," I said and I shifted the Cabriolet into gear. "You've done all you can, the rest is up to me."

Milk Gamble stepped from the automobile, his sack slung over his shoulder. I wrestled with the stubborn steering wheel until I had the Cabriolet turned around. As I headed down the dirt road, I thought about Milk Gamble's words. Soon the road came to an end.

With the Cabriolet parked, I waited as my eyes adjusted to the pale moonlight. A silvery sheen cloaked the world. The tall grass, rocks and trees all glowed with an eerie, iridescent patina. A couple of minutes later, I stepped from the Cabriolet. As I closed the door, I debated upon retrieving the revolver from underneath the seat. I do not know why I had placed it there. It had belonged to my father, so I suppose in a peculiar fashion it was a keepsake, even though it had been useless to him the one time he had needed it. I rolled the notion over and decided against it. I was more likely to hurt myself than anyone or anything else.

In the gloom chirruping crickets and the shrill cries of night birds echoed. Ahead of me rose a steep hillside with a topping of spruces, elms, oaks and maples, each gleaming with the same strange silver radiance.

Milk Gamble had said Rawhide and Bloodybones dwelled here, but he hadn't specified a location. I realized his claim was doubtful — okay, darn right impossible. I didn't expect these ghostly figures to have corporeal forms. I wasn't looking for bogeymen or ghosts. Yet, I wasn't sure about what I was looking for. I simply knew that something was here. I could feel it. Something about this hoary mountain spoke to me.

I started up the mountainside. The steep climb was arduous, particularly for a city fellow. But it gave me plenty of time to mull over the day. I pondered over what Rachel's mother had said and how Rachel had been found, aimlessly wandering in a field. And then I had an epiphany.

Downtown Jefferson rested on the other side of the mountain. Had the sun been shining, a person standing on the top would see the entire city sprawling below, including Jefferson High School. And that was the key. This knowledge had been a knotted mess in the back of my mind all along, tugging me to this place. This mountain was a shortcut from Jefferson High to the Hampton house. A shortcut that a young, adventurous girl might take in place of a school bus, on a hot spring day.

I hurried my pace. I figured a footpath probably cut across the mountain, and it would be easier to spot it from the top. And as I climbed, I came across something else.

My ears registered the sound before the sensation had had time to climb from my foot to my brain. And once my heart had slowed to mild gallop, I spied the object I had kicked in my hurried march. It had an ethereal quality. Pinpoints of moonlight glistened on its surface. An empty, pint-sized liquor bottle. But it wasn't the liquor bottle that held my attention; rather, it was the mound of rocks against which I had kicked the bottle. A man-shaped mound with a bloated hand extending from it, fingers splayed as though reaching to the heavens.

My stomach tightened. I approached the mound warily. Though I willed my feet to move, each step was a struggle as though I were mired in mud. I drew closer. Between the piled rocks I could see a man's face. I dropped to my knees weak with nausea. Though most of his face was revealed, I did not recognize him. I wondered if God himself would recognize him in this surreal light and decayed condition.

With effort I crawled away. I struggled to breathe, and I knew it wasn't because of my discovery. Somehow I knew that Rachel had made the same discovery. And worse. She had discovered the murderer as well. I can't explain where this knowledge came from. I didn't know then, and I still don't. But none-the-less it was there, inside me, burning and filling me full of sickness. And it had been in Rachel's distant, pitiful countenance, too. A shadow of what she had seen, of what she knew.

After several moments I rose to my feet and started down the mountainside. Milk Gamble had been right. Rawhide and Bloodybones had been here.

* * *

That night I had intended to drive straight to Sheriff Harlan's house. But by the time I had entered Jefferson I had changed my mind. If Doctor Clayton's diagnosis had been guided by fear, as I had suspected, then maybe I should consider the matter carefully before charging in like an errant knight on a quest.

The next morning I awoke early from a troubled sleep. In my dreams I had journeyed to a dark, haunting place. It had been a world filled with the dead and dying. It was an old dream. One that was familiar to me from my childhood. The lingering images drove me out of bed.

In a daze I wandered the house debating upon what to do. After an hour or so, I decided on another approach. I would let the solution find me. That had worked before. All I had to do was continue my usual routine, and wait for the answer to germinate and sprout from the depths of my mind. Or so I had hoped.

At 9:30 I drove to Leithem's General Store to do my weekly shopping. Though I wasn't honestly in the mood, I discovered there was little else I could do successfully.

But as the Cabriolet chugged into the gravel lot behind Leithem's, I realized my problems were about to grow.

I admit, I momentarily considered turning around and hightailing it home. And maybe I should have . . . but I didn't. No, I parked the Cabriolet, as I had every Saturday morning since I had lived in Jefferson, and I readied myself.

At the other end of the parking lot, bent beneath the hood of a '27 Model T was Angus Dunne. He had butchered the old vehicle into a truck of sorts. The entire rear had been removed and replaced with a wooden bed that Angus used for hauling. The contraption had almost entirely been pieced together from scrounged parts. The vehicle itself was a testimony to Angus' crafty ingenuity. He dedicated more time to repairing it than to riding in it.

Angus Dunne and I were of two different breeds. I sometimes think that all of the bits and pieces of Angus were glued together with animosity. He cared little for anyone. With most people, he was plain mean. With a Yankee English teacher, Angus was evil.

Yet, I always remained pleasant with the man. Partly because I had hoped to wear him down, and partly because he had fifty pounds and four inches on me.

That morning I had hoped to pass Angus unseen. But that wasn't to be. No sooner had I stepped from the Cabriolet then Angus bellowed.

"Do ya know a'thing 'bout engines, Weaver?"

Though I did, I also knew enough not to say so. For the nearly nine months I had lived in Jefferson, Angus had asked the same question every time he saw me. I'm sure it was my answer that always delighted him.

"No. Absolutely nothing, Angus." As I spoke, I didn't look his way. I simply continued to walk. A misplaced glance with a man like Angus could have the same effect as waving a red cloth in front of a bull.

"Figur'd not," he snorted.

Out of the corner of my eye I saw him pull his head from the mouth of his creation. As I had said, you don't look at a man like Angus unless you're looking for trouble. Yet, a man like Angus you always need to watch. And even without looking at him and my blurry vision, I could discern Angus' gestures and motions. They were grand, bold and confident. Movements not of a common man, but of a king. And from the extreme of my view, I watched Angus Dunne pull a pint-sized bottle from a pocket in his overalls and hoist it to his mouth.

I froze in place, unable to take another step forward. My feet had taken root, and it seemed all I could do on that hot morning of May 26th, 1934 was stand there and watch Angus Dunne out of the corner of my eye.

When I finally managed to turn and face Angus, I saw him gawking at me in pure amazement. His interest in the engine had burned away. Man and lion had met for the first time.

His small, oily eyes made a complete circuit of me. Then he lifted the bottle once again and took a deep swig, keeping his eyes hard set upon me. He returned the bottle to his pocket and began to laugh, revealing a sparse line of yellow, stubby teeth.

"Take a gander at this side-show," he said as the laugh came to a boil in his thick throat. "Do ya have someth'n' to say or are ya jus' dumb?"

The morning sun was hot on my face, and the air was dry. I desperately fought to understand what I was doing. I searched for an explanation, a reason, but there was no adequate answer. No sane rationalization.

I turned and walked to the Cabriolet.

My shoes crunched against the gravel; my legs moved, carrying me forward, yet I was not there, I was in some distant world watching.

"Have a change of heart?" Angus roared. "That's okay, we'll get 'nother chance." I wondered if he would ever understand the grim irony of his words.

My hand popped open the Cabriolet's door. Leaning in, I stretched beneath the seat, my fingers searching like the antennae of an insect. They came upon cold steel. I closed my hand around the revolver, and lifted it into the sunlight.

Angus' full attention had returned to his engine. His bulging torso pressed against the vehicle causing it to rock when he stretched inside deep. Curses and clanks poured from the compartment. When my shadow replaced the morning light, his head cocked toward me, and his barren smile returned to its resting place.

"I'll be damned," he said, pulling himself free of the engine. His face and neck were greasy with sweat.

I raised the revolver.

The darkness that dwelled in his eyes intensified. The dilapidated smile vanished as his jaw clenched. Muscles in his neck moved beneath his slick skin, tensing and relaxing and tensing. And then I saw it.

It was the same as my dream. Darkness. Writhing people. Women, men, mothers, fathers, children all smothering and drowning and burning and dying. It had been there all along, plain and simple, only I had refused to see it. I saw them. And I saw what they had done to Angus. And for the first time, I saw what they had done to me.

I now know that Rawhide and Bloodybones are bogeymen. And you cannot hide from them. If you try, they'll sneak up and steal away a part of you. And they'll keep doing it until there is nothing left. You cannot run from them, either. Once they've touched you, you *are* stained forever.

"Better get me with one shot," he said. "'Cause there ain't gonna be 'nother chance."

"I know about the man buried on the mountain."

His eyes seemed to soften as though recalling a fond memory, then they shifted from my face to the revolver and back again.

"Whadd'ya jabber'n 'bout?" he said.

"I know about the girl. I know what you did to her."

His face rounded with a malignant pleasure, eyes folding, lips pursing, then it abruptly vanished.

"That little strumpet! What did she say?" he roared.

My finger tightened on the trigger. Silence flooded the world. And then it all ended unceremoniously with the sound of the revolver.

Click.

"That was yer one chance," he growled with evil delight.

Angus lunged forward, knocked my hand aside and hurled his mass against me. I went down. The impact pushed the air from my lungs and sent a twisting pain crawling madly through my body, exploring every bone and joint. The morning sky began to fade.

Angus worked with diligence, determination and glee. Hunkered down with his weight pinning me, he hammered iron fists against my head.

With each second the world grew more abstract. In the distance I could feel his bulky fingers prying at my hand, miles away from the rest of me. Effortlessly he snapped my fingers back, breaking bones as he proceeded.

"Time for a lesson," he said, pulling the revolver from my hand.

I heard the cylinder snap open and click back into place before his weight lifted from my body. Through a dark haze, I saw Angus take aim. Then he convulsed, his chest exploded and he dropped to the ground.

"How bad hurt are ya, Mr. Weaver?" Though it took some moments, I recognized the voice of Sheriff Harlan. I thought about his question. I thought about my answer. Then I said, "I'm alive."

* * *

There had been one more week of school, that year. And though I looked like something a dog had buried and dug-up, I managed to finish the semester. It would take a long time for me to heal — though my fingers still ache to this day, and they're not as nimble as they used to be.

It seems that during my scuffle with Angus quite a crowd had gathered around us, including Sheriff Harlan. Unfortunately for Angus, the audience had entered mid-story, so to speak, so they hadn't seen the event unfold from the beginning. Afterward, Sheriff Harlan told me that he had called off Angus, but the man hadn't listened. Angus had a reputation for being a touch bullheaded, so it didn't surprise most people. But, Sheriff Harlan said when Angus lifted the revolver, he had no choice but to shoot Angus. I decided to let the story stand with the addition of my mountaintop discovery. The Sheriff didn't care to press much further.

I said nothing about Rachel.

Rachel returned to school on the last day of class. She looked tired, and sadness seemed to be lurking around the edges of her mouth.

And on that last day, Rachel remained behind after I had dismissed the class. Hesitantly she approached my desk. It was the first time I had seen her in dungarees. Cradled in her arms were several books.

"How are you feeling, Mr. Weaver?" Her voice was as soft and delicate as a rose petal.

"I'm well," I said. "How are you?"

"I'm okay." She extracted a thin volume from her collection. "I want to thank you for leaving this," she said, placing it on my desk.

I reached forward with my good hand and pulled the book toward me. "I'm pleased you enjoyed it. It's an old story, and a bit outdated."

She smiled and her face seemed to brighten a little. Then she turned and walked to the door.

I examined the old book. The cover was worn and the binding loose. For a moment, a brief moment, I fancied giving it to

Rachel as a gift. But I could see that it was too old and worn.

That was my last year at Jefferson. I returned to Chicago that summer.

* * *

"That's it?" Charlie Hopkins asked.

I chuckled. "For the most part."

As I had neared the middle of my tale, I had seen Charlie Hopkins check his watch. He was still holding out, hoping for a chance himself.

"I don't think we'll be hearing any more stories today," Emma said. The rest of the room nodded in silent agreement.

Even Vera was quiet. Normally she made a comment or two about the stories, or in the least asked questions. I had half-expected a few loose corners that needed to be stretched or tucked in my tale, but she said nothing. Rather, the expression she wore resembled the leery and uncertain look a person might give a dog with a reputation for biting.

Once again my mirth bubbled over and a short chuckle escaped me.

As the members of our club slowly and solemnly began to vacate the community room, I settled in a spot by the windows. The warmth of the sun felt good, and it helped me to think.

"How are you feeling, Lloyd?" Emma asked, letting the others move ahead.

"Good," I said. "Darn good." It had been a number of years since I had taught a class, but the feeling was as I had remembered it.

She nodded knowingly and proceeded.

I leaned back and I wondered about my next anniversary. You never know what will turn up. Just about every day is an anniversary, if you have a head for it.

FEASTERS OF THE DARK

"Here rests the noblest of all human endeavors, and its rankest, most wretched secrets. In New York City, I see mankind's greatest hope, or the last spark of divinity forever extinguished. What will those who judge us decide?"

—Rudolph Pearson

I CLIMBED THE SEESAWING stairs of the fusty tenement building, only reaching the fourth floor after much arduous effort. The dimly lighted hallways and sullen doors kept me close on the heels of Detective Matthew Leahy. Being a professor of literature, I seldom frequented the darker places of New York City, or participated in any form of strenuous exercise beyond the carrying of texts — though there are a few works I do indeed consider strenuous in bulk and content.

"Dr. Pearson, you may want a moment to prepare yourself," Leahy said as we ended our expedition before an apartment door. Flanking this scarred and worn portal stood two placid uniformed officers.

Detective Leahy himself was a stocky man with thick black hair, not too dissimilar to the officers. Unlike them, though, an ill-fitting gray-wool suit covered his bulk, combined with sharp features and slow, seemingly calculated movements, making him reminiscent of a turtle toting about a cumbersome shell. This image, however, I found was quickly dispelled by his alert blue eyes that were always taking in the world around him.

"This is an–" The detective halted abruptly, not for lack of a proper word, but as a man might catch himself before putting forth a remark in which he did not fully and earnestly believe. His expression grew dark as though he had stepped from light into shadow. I had the distinct impression that he felt there was no accurate means of describing what lay beyond the doorway.

"It is unusual," he finally concluded.

I was grateful for the brief lull, which allowed me a moment to catch my breath. As I stood huffing, I was certain I spotted a twinkle of amusement in the eyes of the previously stoic officers. A Columbia University professor at the scene of a murder likely did seem ludicrous to these gentlemen, who most probably thought me nothing more than a mollycoddle. In honesty, it seemed such to myself. Had not Detective Leahy convinced me of the necessity for a literary scholar, I most assuredly would have thought my presence nothing more than a fancy, only likely to appear in the countless commercial literature plaguing the publishing houses nowadays.

Instead, I struggled to make my attendance seem commonplace, matter-of-fact, as if professors of English regularly patrolled New York City's streets enforcing good grammar, lecturing upon the literary canon, and solving crimes.

"I understand," I replied firmly. Then I committed myself to a course that would gnaw at my very soul for the remainder of my life.

As I followed Detective Leahy through the door, I realized I did *not* understand. I had no comprehension of what I was seeing, or its greater meaning.

The apartment was divided into two small rooms. There was neither a private bath nor room enough for anything more than the smallest of beds.

"This—" Leahy gestured toward a dark corner of the modest room. "This is where the landlord found the victim's body. His remains are being held at the medical examiner's office at the Bellevue Pavilion."

Reflexively, I withdrew a handkerchief and placed it to my face. The sickly sweet odor of dried blood permeated the room, making the already small space feel as immuring as a coffin. A single light bulb dangled from the ceiling, casting a wan light, making tall shadows on all of the walls, leaving the close corners of the room dark and gloomy.

I stepped forward, halting before a black stain that stretched from part of the floor to the wall. The discoloration extended toward the ceiling as though the blood had climbed upward with a life of its own.

"The way in which the blood has splattered on the wall," Leahy said, "indicates the victim, a Russian immigrant named Adrik Ziven, was killed at this spot." The detective extracted an electric torch from his overcoat and shone it upon the location. A circle of light danced in the grisly corner. "This is what I wanted you to see."

I followed the light as it sliced through the shadows along the wall, revealing letters scrawled there. They were thick and ill-formed, writhing like snakes, obviously written in blood.

I studied the dark scribbling, immediately recognizing the words, though not wanting to confront their meaning. After scanning the ghastly writing several times, I read it aloud: "*Lætan riht onfindan þæt scyldig.*"

Leahy looked at me expectantly.

"It is as you suspected," I said. "A form of English. Specifically, a corrupted version of Old English. It translates to 'Let justice discover the guilty.'"

I continued. "*He gearwian þæt fyllo man hwa forlætan se leoht.* He serves the feast for those who have abandoned the light."

I turned away, hoping vainly that not seeing the words would distance their meaning from me. "How was Ziven killed?" I asked, a cloying nausea burning in my throat.

"The medical examiner believes he was eaten alive." Leahy moved to the wall, still shining his torch. "These high stains indicate arterial splashes . . ."

I raised a hand, interrupting him. The dreadful message already conveyed more detail than I desired.

"I apologize, Dr. Pearson," Leahy said. "My senses have grown dull to such horrors. In time, it all becomes puzzle pieces and nothing more. You must become inhuman to solve inhuman crimes."

As Leahy spoke, the memory of a text I had studied years ago came unbidden to my mind. It was a medieval text about religion, demons and devils. The part I suddenly recollected was identical to what I had just read on the wall. *He serves the feast for those who have abandoned the light.*

It seemed unfathomable that a fiend capable of such an act would also be a connoisseur of medieval literature. I tried to convince myself that my mind was playing tricks on me; my unsettled state was causing morbid fancies, nothing more.

"What was Ziven's occupation?" I asked, attempting to divert my thoughts from their dark course.

"He was a petty thief and robber. Sentenced to three years at Blackwell's. Insignificant when compared to many others in his field." The detective shrugged his shoulders. "He must have made a bad enemy somewhere along the line."

I looked at Leahy. "Then maybe this message is an epitaph for Ziven?"

"Or a challenge to the law," Leahy countered.

"Have you consulted an alienist? Perhaps he may be able to shed light upon these writings?"

"I already have, even though it was pointless." There was sharpness in Leahy's words. "There are few alienists who care to diagnose absentee patients. Most are interested in injecting drugs and applying straight jackets. They have little to gain from speculating about messages on walls in tenement houses, and often do not consider the death of such a man as Ziven a crime at all. What the alienist did tell me —" Leahy gestured to the wall — "was that he thought this to be Old English." The detective moved toward the wall, his gaze intent upon the mystery before him.

I could see passion in his eyes. To understand the meaning of this riddle gave him a purpose, a significance; it separated him from the senselessness of the crime itself. It provided him with the semblance of meaning in a world where meaning was often absent. I knew this because I too felt the need to understand tugging at me. The riddle on the wall called to me like it did Leahy. The meaning and purpose behind those words, in conjunction with such an unimaginable act, attracted me like iron to a lodestone.

I watched him scrutinize the wall for several moments before I spoke. "I believe I can assist you."

* * *

I returned to my office at Columbia University by taxicab to scour my notes. I had hoped to find a hint or clue in my records that might lead me to the medieval text of which I had earlier been reminded.

I pored over volumes, notes and lists of references I maintained for research. I have always despised thumbing through endless cards in a catalog in pursuit of a text; so I developed, like most professors, a highly specialized list of commonly used and referenced works. This tack soon proved unproductive, forcing me to continue my research at the university library.

The library's card catalog guarded the main entrance. Like the Sphinx, it sat silent and knowing, fat with knowledge, reluctant to disgorge even the slightest tidbit. I loathed the thing and needed it all at once, a horrible irony for any scholar, and doubly so in my eyes.

Reluctantly I set to work. My desire to understand the meaning of the writing in the tenement overpowered my hatred for "thumbwork." I focused my search upon the darker writings of the medieval period, the superstitious manuals about demons and devils and witchcraft.

Tedious hours passed as I skimmed countless volumes, many long forgotten or dismissed by scholars. Endless pages given life with words by dead authors worried my eyes. Eventually I set upon a curious text by Henry Hollowell — a pendant of whom I knew nothing.

The book was titled *Divine Feasts*, and was published in 1914. It described an medieval grimoire that Hollowell claimed to be lost, and most likely destroyed by the church. That book was titled *Haes of Gowles*. According to Hollowell this hoary and quite elusive tome held an account of an obscure monastic order that drastically deviated from their Christian doctrine. This handful of monks practiced heretical rituals and spoke of fantastical creatures that lived in the bowels of the Earth. Years of pursuit by the church forced the monks into caverns and the deep places of the world only they knew existed. The surface was shunned, they ventured out only in darkness to steal away humans upon whom they feasted.

The cannibalism, Hollowell theorized, transformed these gruesome monks into creatures that resembled an unnatural mixture of humans and canines. And he stated that this very same diet also extended their lives far beyond the years of the oldest humans. The practice apparently was an element of their rituals; for the monks believed that they were devouring the evil of humanity, absolving mankind of its sins. Each ceremonial feast concluded with the writing of sacred phrases in the sinner's blood. I must confess, for many moments I was unhinged by what I read next:

Let justice discover the guilty. He serves the feast for those who have abandoned the light. We cleanse the path for those not of darkness. Our hunger consumes the flesh that sins. In us, the lost shall find a living Hell.

Although I cannot be certain, I now believe there is at least one copy of *Haes of Gowles* in existence. And it is held at the Oxford library in England. That is where I did my undergraduate studies, and that is where I believe I had previously read those putrescent words.

I do not know how long I stood there, frozen in place, grabbing the book in my hands, fingers clenching the pages. When I had recovered sufficiently, I carried the volume to a table, where I feverishly went to work copying the sections I believed most significant.

Word for word I hurriedly scribbled, not bothering to translate, fearing something might be lost in my rush. My attention was so intense, so focused, that I lost all awareness of the world around me. My only means of perceiving how many hours had passed was the blurriness in my vision, and the remonstrations of Miss Webber, a persnickety librarian, who doggedly reminded me that all rare texts must be returned to the desk thirty minutes before closing.

When I had finished I was astounded, or perhaps horrified, to see how closely my scrawl resembled the script on the tenement wall. The likeness unleashed a horde of scurrying chills across my flesh.

✱ ✱ ✱

When I returned with Leahy to Ziven's tenement on the Lower

East Side, a vault of darkness covered the city. As we rolled down the street in his department purchased Chevrolet, anemic yellow light glowered from the narrow tenement windows like incandescent warning signs.

"You think this book is related to the murder?" Leahy asked, still trying to sort out the details in my hurried explanation.

"No," I replied. "The book explains — possibly explains — the writing." I wasn't yet ready to commit to any theory. Too often in my career I have learned that reality and theory do not meet; and in my present, frazzled state of mind, I wanted to avoid any sort of commitment, permanent or temporary. Yet, there was something about it that smacked of truth, a fearsome truth that I could not ignore. I needed to peer behind the curtain of reality to see what dark secrets lurked there, unknown to those of us going about our mundane lives.

"The book describes a religious cult," I said. "A cult that practiced cannibalism. The words on the wall belong to one of their ceremonies."

Leahy steered the automobile into an alleyway. "Eating people is part of their religion?" he asked skeptically.

"They consume the flesh of . . . sinners."

"I see," he said. "So if this is true, why haven't I heard of this gang before? There are many murders in New York each year, but this is the first act of cannibalism I know of."

Although I did not attempt to change Leahy's mind, I suspected there had been others in the past. Either they went unnoticed or had gone unmentioned. I feared with the continuing growth of the city's population, he would certainly see more in the future. And at that moment I was struck with a terrifying realization.

New York City was rapidly expanding skyward in an attempt to accommodate the immense hoard of urban denizens within its borders. Each day a new, taller building was erected. Apartment houses and hotels reached toward the heavens, overflowing with residents. But upward was not the only direction the city was expanding.

Without uttering a word of this to Leahy, I stepped from the automobile into the murky alleyway. Leahy promptly followed, asking about my intentions.

It took some convincing, but I eventually coaxed the detective into assisting me with the removal of a manhole cover I found behind Zevin's tenement.

With a muted *clank* we pulled the heavy cover from its snug fitting. The exercise appeared to have little if any effect upon Leahy; while I found myself dabbing a handkerchief at beads of perspiration gathered on my brow.

"What do you think is down there?" Leahy asked, shining his electric torch into the depths of the glistening shaft.

"I pray nothing. My hope is that I am reading far too much into this entire episode."

He pointed the torch to my chest so it would cast a dim light upon my visage. With his face steeped in shadows, unseen to me, I could feel his hard eyes settling upon me.

"You sure you're up to this?" he asked. His words were anxious — not from fear, however. He too could feel the puzzle drawing us below. No matter how adamantly either of us denied the sanity of our actions, we both sensed an answer awaited us.

"I don't think waiting will prepare me any better," I said, then proceeded to climb into the sewer.

Cautiously I gripped the rusted and slimy rungs anchored into the walls. Leahy followed, the light clamped in one hand.

A fetid stench awaited us at the bottom of the ladder, as did a dark stream of water.

"Which way?" Leahy asked, his voice bouncing off the stony walls, mingling with the plop and drip and splash of water. He guided the light down both ends of the passage. They continued endlessly.

"This way," I ventured a guess and started to walk.

"Hold up there," Leahy ordered. "Let me take the front." He produced a revolver. "I'm better prepared in case we do find someone."

The passage was narrow, forcing both of us to crouch as we slogged along. I did my best not to think of the ankle-deep water that flooded my shoes and turned my socks into disgusting mires of damp cloth.

The further we drudged into the watery darkness, the more the place took on the appearance of a labyrinth. Here and there new tunnels intersected, stretching into blackness. With each intersection, Leahy slowed, waiting for me to offer guidance. After a while, he understood there was no method to my navigation and began selecting the direction himself.

The farther we delved, the more oppressive the putrid atmosphere became. A need to feel open air began to boil and churn inside me. I fought against the urge to flee back the way I came and return to the familiar embrace of the surface.

Just as I was about to suggest we abandon the sewer, I heard a strange cry, a sound akin to that made by a startled person. It was shrill and sharp, but brief. I could not discern if a man or a woman made it, a child or an adult. It was so . . . unusual that I wasn't sure it came from a human at all.

Immediately Leahy halted, his stocky frame blocking my progress. He quickly cast the light about, searching all directions. As he turned to shine it behind us, I heard another sound. This time it was a guttural gibbering of sorts. A sense of rhythm and structure. I knew it was a language. But I did not recognize it in the least.

Within a few seconds there was another gibbering, this time more distant and urgent. It was clear the sounds were coming from behind us.

"Stay here," Leahy said, dashing off after the sounds.

Before I could protest, Leahy bounded down the slimy corridor, quickly darting into a side passage, bringing all the light in the world with him. I found myself in absolute and total darkness.

Standing there, alone, in festering water, I listened intently for any new sound. My hearing seemed almost supernatural, for in the darkness I could now hear rats gnawing at the refuse, cockroaches scuttling across the old and weary stone, and the worms wriggling in the silt and slime beneath my feet.

The desire of open air burned in my brain. I dug in my pocket, feeling for a matchbox, hoping to relieve the building pressure of the darkness. Fumbling blindly, I fiddled out a match and snapped it to life.

The small flame that danced on the match-head seemed insignificant against the menacing curtain of blackness that threatened to enshroud me.

Anxiously I squinted and peered into the surrounding void, hoping to glimpse Leahy's lantern. I carefully moved in the direction he'd bolted, taking only a few steps before the match flickered out. Ghosts of the flame lingered in my vision for several moments before they too vanished, leaving me in a deeper darkness than I had ever before known.

With greater urgency, I lit another match, and found something other than Leahy. It was beyond my imagination; beyond the conception of the fiction I had dedicated my life to studying. It was utterly *unreal* because it was all too real. *Too, too sullied flesh.*

My blood chilled. My muscles froze. I was unable to cry out or flee in panic. I simply stood as still as a statue, brandishing a tiny flame in one hand.

Icy yellow eyes gazed upon me. Their fearful owner slouched low, its rangy arms dangling at its flanks. The sickly light of the match revealed a flesh of greenish tint, and a visage that had a nose and mouth that seemingly formed a muzzle.

I fully expected it to lurch forward, eyes wide with hunger, sharp teeth ready to rend flesh. But like myself, it remained in place, shifting from one foot to another in its low crouch.

The match burned low, scorching my finger and thumb. I instinctively waved it out and began to strike another.

"No," a rasping voice said. "No light."

I returned the matchbox to my jacket pocket.

"All right," I said congenially, hoping not to agitate it.

Moments passed without an utterance. Although I could not see the creature, I pictured it rocking from side-to-side before me. The image was unbearable. All I could do to quench the impulse to flee was to speak.

"Who are you?" I asked.

"Ad . . . rik," it hesitated as if stumbling of the words. "Adrik . . . Zi-ven."

"That's not possible. Ziven is dead."

The creature meeped and gurgled for several seconds, as though it too were subduing some urge.

"Not . . . dead," it finally said. "Ch-changed."

"Changed how?" I asked.

Before answering I heard its mouth smack as though it

needed to contend with a growing pool of saliva. "Consumed," it uttered flatly. "He is in me," the creature continued, its words swollen. "I consumed his memories . . . knowledge."

I remembered Hollowell's book and his claims. His theories had become my reality. It was electrifying and repulsive at the same time. My mind spun at the knowledge contained in this creature, and others like it. It was a living library, replete with the lost secrets and memories of humanity.

"How many people have you . . . changed?" I asked, anxiously.

"Many . . . many . . . many inside me."

"Are there others here like you?"

"Yesss." I heard a wetness in its answer as though it were losing a Pavlovian battle. "We are many. We have always been here. Your secrets draw us. Change us. Give us life."

My mind whirled. I was consumed by thoughts of discovery. This creature's knowledge and abilities could shape the destiny of humanity.

"Why do you hide?" I asked. "I — we — could help you. We could share knowledge."

The reply came in the form of a swampy hiss. "Nooo. We eat your secrets," it said harshly. "Sins . . . we consume your sins. The light is not ours."

With this confession, cold sanity returned to me. I was standing before a creature who was a repository of humanity's evil, a living collection of mankind's atrocities and dark secrets. It lived in a world of bounteous feasts, and possessed an insatiable hunger.

I could hear it slavering. I imagined long ropes of drool oozing from its muzzle. Terror burned inside my mind, fired by the realization I was its next feast.

In an instant I bolted from my spot. I ran blindly through the darkness, hoping against hope that I would stumble upon an exit from these loathsome tunnels. With each step my heart raced, pounding against my chest. My movements felt sluggish. With every stride, I sensed the vile creature on my trail.

I do not know how far I had fled before I slipped. Looking back, I now realize it was inevitable. The slick, uneven floors, crooked and cracked from age, were difficult to cross in the light. But in complete darkness, there was no hope.

With a single misplaced step, I tumbled forward, splashing in the tainted water, flailing to upright myself. Each time I reached out, my hand returned with a disgusting handful of sewage. I crawled on my hands and knees, searching for an outlet. Unable to bear the darkness any longer, I reached into my jacket pocket and retrieved my matches. The box had miraculously avoided being doused. Hastily I fumbled with the matchbox, spilling matches as I delved for a single one. When I snatched it from the box, I heard the splashing nearby.

I gasped for breath, gulping the foul air, choking with every breath. Fearing my huffing would extinguish my solitary hope for light, I clamped my mouth shut, fighting my instinct to breathe. I snapped the match against my thumb, hearing a reassuring pop of the chemical head. A blinding light and a thunderous roar followed this. Flames filled the sewer, flaring in all directions.

For an instant I felt the burning tongues of Hell lapping at my flesh. Then I found oblivion.

When consciousness returned, it came turgidly and painfully, in the form of slow needle pokes. The pain eventually blossomed into a biting sharpness, shifting along my arms and legs. The world remained dark.

I was certain a pack of ravenous creatures were stooped over me, feeding upon my flesh. Unable to endure this bleak fate, I screamed a pitiful cry. I screamed until my lungs ached. I struggled to upright myself, but insidious paws pressed me down.

"Rudolph," I heard someone utter my name. "Rudolph, be calm. All is well."

It seemed as though an eternity passed before I recognized the voice. It was Effram Harris, a dear friend of mine, and professor of physics at Columbia.

"You are at the hospital, Rudolph. The doctors are treating you for minor burns. They say you ignited a methane pocket in a sewer." I felt his hand press against my shoulder. "You really should read a few more books on chemistry if you intend to go prowling the city's sewers."

I flinched at Effram's touch, not from of pain, but from the memory of fear, it coursed through me like a poison. I brought a hand to my eyes, feeling the bandages covering them.

"Those are only temporary," Effram assured me. "You'll be reading your books in no time."

"What about Leahy?" I asked, my voice as raspy as the creature I encountered in the sewer.

"He is safe. He found you. He said you were assisting him with a case, the details of which he was not permitted to disclose." Effram snorted. "Everyone has a secret. You will have to tell me this story sometime. I'm very anxious to learn how you became tangled up with a police detective, Rudolph. But for now, the doctors want you to rest."

I heard a chair scrape against the floor. "I must return to the university to update the faculty," Effram said. "I'll be back tomorrow. Get some rest."

I lay in the bed for sometime after Effram had departed, marveling at how Leahy and I had miraculously survived — and no doubt how the creatures had also survived. I was certain they were still in the shadows below the city, feeding off humanity's malevolence, waiting for their next feast. This was the answer for which I so desperately had been searching since I read the words on the wall. There was no satisfaction to be had from this dark knowledge. It only offered horror and despair. And there was nothing I could do to erase it from my mind, no way of ridding my soul of this foulness. It would always be present, lurking inside me, burrowing its black tendrils deeper into my brain. Forever changing me. How long? I wondered. How long before all the sins of humanity — all of humanity — are consumed and find a new life inside the feasters of the dark?

A Change of Life

I WATCHED AS HANNAH glided down the flagstone path that twisted through the Trinity Church cemetery. She had the grace of a majestic bird in flight, and somehow managed to appear furtive as a mouse who had just spied the shadow of a hawk flying overhead.

Early spring has always been one of my favorite seasons. And New York City in early spring was a delightful place to visit. Even in 1929, when the financial district was booming, its streets swarming with people, and a vista of dizzying skyscrapers surrounding the district, it somehow still seemed welcoming. So, I was pleased to find myself sitting on the stone bench at the Trinity Church Cemetery. Although the majority of my company were less lively than I was accustomed to; even the living ones were stern faced bankers and brokers on their lunch break. Nonetheless it was pleasant. *Serene.* Yes.

As Hannah approached me, a tight, nervous smile flitted across her face. She was clad in a high-collared jacket and pleated skirt, both of a deep red hue. Her hair was silky black and cropped short, with a defiant cowlick that could only exist south of Chelsea.

Her apprehensive glimpses around the blossoming trees and lush grass of the cemetery were not directed toward the other *living* occupants. She was looking for someone less obvious.

The city had grown taller since my last visit. I marveled at the numerous buildings reaching toward the heavens, and the number still under construction, each trying to soar higher than the next. I wondered what *thing* drove such marvelous creations. What tortured lives humanity must live that they needed to construct such marvels.

When Hannah reached me, she stood a moment without speaking; she simply gazed at me as though she wasn't sure she recognized me now that she was closer. In the background, traffic growled along Broadway.

"Hello, Mickey," Hannah eventually said. Looking toward the sharp blue sky and the fiery visage hanging directly above, she added, "It is a nice day for a trip."

"It is," I replied. "Most certainly."

Realizing a brown paper bag was perched alongside me on the bench — I assumed it was my lunch — I snatched it up, clearing a spot for her. The paper crackled, and it seemed unusually heavy for a lunch.

Hannah lowered herself onto the bench. "So what do we do next?"

I thought about the question a moment, letting memories slowly float to the surface. It was a good question.

"We need to get you to Penn Station," I said after a moment.

"Are you feeling all right, Mickey?" Hannah asked, placing one of her delicate hands upon my shoulder. "You don't look like your usual self. You're . . . quiet and still."

I could tell she longed for a better word than "still," but apparently it eluded her.

But she was correct. I did recall being a little more energetic, and much more boisterous. And no, I didn't feel altogether myself, but I knew that would pass.

"I'm fine," I said. "I'm just not feeling myself today."

Again a cautious expression flashed across her face. It was brief, for she quickly regained her composure. Although, now her voice was no longer soft. There was a slight edge to it.

"I thought we were going to take the ferry to New Jersey," she said. "Why have you changed your mind?"

I shrugged. "Instinct, I guess. Besides, Penn Station is crowded. It's a better place. From there you can head South."

Hannah knotted her hands together. Turning from me to face the back of the Church. "I'm not so sure I should do this,

Mickey. I mean Dutch has been good to me. Maybe I can just explain it. Apologize. He'll forgive me."

Even through the tension in her voice, I could hear the beauty in it, the melodious nature. The voice of a singer, an artist. I then recalled her singing in one of Dutch's smoky Speakeasies.

The memories were returning quicker now. You might say I was feeling more like my old self. "You know better than that, Hannah," I said. "No one nabs fifty long ones from Dutch Schultz and walks away. Sure, Dutch will smile and say it is all right, but then he'll send someone for you."

I wondered if my vernacular was hyperbolic. I always had the greatest difficulty adjusting to human slang. It was a slippery element of human language, always changing meaning like the seasons. It was inefficient, and allowed for spurious interpretations.

Her deep green eyes cast toward me. There was a question in them. At first I thought I had uttered something that gave me away. But then I caught her eye darting at the brown paper bag in my lap. I realized why the bag was so heavy.

"It's not me," I said. "Well, it *was*. But it ain't no more. Dutch sent me to do the job. But I ain't." Like trying on a new glove, it sometimes took a while to break it in. I was slowly getting the feel for Mickey; how he moved, how he talked. It was all coming back.

She smiled. Her countenance softened; her eyes began to well with tears. "I was so afraid it was you," she said. When I saw you, something seemed different. For a moment you weren't the Mickey I knew."

Even for the greatest artist, manipulating human hosts can be risky. From her reaction, it appeared I had overcome the initial unstable period.

I hefted the paper bag in my lap, recognizing the weight of a handgun. My returning memories told me it was a .38 revolver. Clean and simple. Shoot Hannah here, leave, and somewhere along the way ditch the paper bag. No prints, no witnesses to see me with the weapon. Nice, clean and simple. That was how Mickey liked things done. And I was Mickey.

Mickey Guinn, or more affectionately known among the criminal elements of New York City: Mickey "The Gun" Guinn.

"The Gun" had been attached to my host's name because of his habit of never carrying a gun on his person. Instead, he toted his instruments of trade in creative fashions. Today it was a lunch bag, since the Church cemetery was a popular lunch spot in the district. I believed that by not concealing a weapon on me, the cops couldn't nab me for a job. Rather, my host believed that. Sometimes in the early stages of inhabitation, personas tended to blend and overlap. I had inhabited Mickey previously, and knew that there was no part of his personality I wanted blended with mine. So I decided to be very cautious to prevent bleed over.

"I'm still not the Mickey you knew," I said. "But I am the guy you can trust. And right now you need to get to Penn Station in a snap."

The tears continued to well until they overflowed. Hannah leaned over, wrapping her slender arms around my bulky frame. "Thank you," she said, softly. "I knew I could count on you."

On me, but certainly not Mickey Guinn.

I sometimes found it entertaining how human lives transpire. Unlike my species, humans are corporeal beings, temporally fixed into a solitary biochemical construct that is locked into a social and political superstructure that dominates and controls their lives. Or as Mickey would be tempted to put it, "Some people get stuck with rotten luck." Hannah was one of those people.

Like me, she was an artist, a being with a talent. But unlike me, she was unable to practice her art to its fullest extent. She had "rotten luck." Her life was to be played out singing in the Speakeasies of a degenerate, Brooklyn bootlegger who was fond of killing other humans for entertainment.

The contrary occurred in human society as well. Despicable, loathsome men, such as Dutch Schultz, were living lives that circumstance has delivered to them. When I consider it, I rarely come across a human who lives the life he or she deserves. A pitiable species.

"Let's get moving," I said, wiggling from Hannah's embrace. "When I don't return, Dutch will get suspicious."

We worked our way up Broadway, walking against a stream of men in suits going about their daily business. Finding satisfied looks wasn't difficult. The human pastime called "economy" was exceedingly profitable in the spring of 1929. But, that was soon to change. Before the end of the year an economic crash would cast the entire nation into turmoil. This was just one *intervention* arranged by the Great Race; one that would reawaken a war that humanity had thought to be over. This was typical human folly. Since the Armistice of the Great War, the wounds of the world had not healed; they had scabbed over, and were merely festering. The Great Race knew that the collapse of one of humanity's reigning political powers would help re-infect this old wound, spurring a fevered conflict the likes that human history had never seen before. This second world conflict would bring humanity into the atomic age at too early a stage in their development as a species.

Outright genocide was unthinkable by the Great Race. Aeons ago we'd overcome such temptations. Subtlety and power were our tools. There was no need to directly bring about the destruction of humanity; humanity was too desperate to accomplish this task on its own. They just needed proper guidance. And the Great Race of Yith would gladly provide such guidance. The Earth would someday belong to us.

From Broadway we made our way to Park Row, cutting across City Hall Park, another one of Manhattan's verdant oases. *I do so have a fondness of greenery. In the distant future where I dwell, all flora have become extinct.*

Hurriedly I urged Hannah to the Hudson Terminal. I knew Dutch anticipated Hannah's taking the ferry across the bay, so I figured I could buy her some time by heading to Penn Station. The route was circuitous in an attempt to keep any of Dutch's other toughs off our tail.

Intermingling of memories must be avoided.

As we entered the steeple roofed transit terminal, it too, like so many of the city's other structures, was infested with humans. Each one was rushing about, anxious to depart from one location to arrive at another.

"Mickey," Hannah said in a hushed voice as we climbed aboard a subway car. "I have enough for the both of us." She looked at me sheepishly, the slightest glimmer of a blush on her face. "I . . . I don't mean *we* — us as a thing, that is. I mean I can repay you for your help. You can come with me."

I smiled at the offer. She was a gentle human, very much unlike the host I occupied. "You know I can't do that, Hannah," I said. "I'm in. Always will be."

She nodded quickly, then looked away as the subway car began to rattle and shake into motion. Through the windows I watched the Hudson terminal slide past my eyes; but in my mind's eye I saw the past and future of the terminal swirling together. A thick forest sprawled outward, a place where humans of different skin pigmentation battled and killed one another. Flames and fire appeared as colossal buildings collapsed, spewing forth roiling clouds of smoke and debris, killing thousands of humans. This spot, like nearly every spot I visited upon this world, was replete, sated and bloodied with the past and future histories of human conflict. It will be a mercy to these creatures when my species dominates this world. Yet, even without the machinations of the Great Race, and the ingenious plans and interventions calculated to direct and alter human events, it seemed clear that humanity would eventually destroy itself.

Soon we rolled into Penn Station. Waiting for us were more crowds of travelers, each pushing and squeezing through the congested station, all in a race to catch a train out of the city or to hurry into it.

With the money my host carried, I purchased Hannah a ticket to Richmond, Virginia. I thought it was the least my host could do after having planned to betray her.

As we approached the train platform, I noticed Hannah stiffen. During our trip across town, she'd been anxious, but having earned her trust, she had gradually relaxed. Now her wariness returned. I scanned the crowd, looking for the source of her anxiety. Although humans do not have collective minds, I've found their physical reactions often betray their thoughts. Over the centuries of occupying hosts, I have become an excellent reader of the physical human text.

As my eyes skipped across the throng of jelly faced humans inside the train station, my host's body reacted to one in particular. Being non-corporeal, the most difficult part of inhabiting humans was adjusting to the chemical surges produced by their bodies. Everything was stimulated and activated by chemical and electrical impulses. To successfully inhabit a host requires true mastery and artistry. I sometimes lament the inevitable loss of humans because of my extreme talent to manipulate them. But, it is better that humanity is destroyed and the Great Race survive at the sacrifice of my gift.

Within a moment I was able to pull forth the memories connected to the face that triggered the biochemical reaction. I recognized the human known as "Dazzy." He worked for Dutch, and from probing my host's mind, I comprehended that we were associates, although much distrust and animosity thrived in our relationship.

He stood in the crowd, motionless. People flowed around him as though he were a large stone in a swift moving stream. A broad rimmed hat adorned his head, and a gray, pinstriped suit hung over his narrow frame. His eyes almost seemed reptilian, and I detected the slightest squint in them when he saw me.

The text of the human body is a complex book. Reading it is difficult and often susceptible to errors. But, some texts are easier to read than others. And Dazzy was one of the simplest texts I had encountered. From the twitch of his hand to the straightening of his shoulders I could read his intention.

Somewhere during one of my previous inhabitations of my host's body, someone who worked for Dutch, or maybe Dutch himself, must have detected my affection for Hannah, which is why Dazzy was here. Dutch didn't completely trust my host.

"What do we do, Mickey?" Hannah asked, her voice beginning to tremble.

"You board the train. I'll speak with Dazzy."

Hannah hesitated for a moment, apparently unsure about the plausibility of my suggestion.

"Do it, Han!" I yelled.

Dazzy shook his head as though reprimanding me; then he slowly shifted toward me.

Even to the dullest of the humans in the station, it was obvious that this was not a safe location.

A hush washed over the thinning crowd. People backed away. At first their movement was sluggish, uncertain. Then as they realized what was unfolding between Dazzy and me, they began to scurry away.

Being a master of the study of human psychology, I was certain that in Dazzy's mind time had slowed. Or more accurately stated, Dazzy *believed* time had slowed down. This, of course, was nothing more than a misperception. The Great Race were the masters of time and physics. Humanity had only the faintest concepts of these matters, and it was the Great Race who implanted those limited notions into the minds of humanity's greatest scientists in order that they might develop atomic weapons and bring about self-destruction. *Infants with toys.*

Time held no sway over me. This left Dazzy at a manifest disadvantage in the game he was about to play.

But Dazzy didn't see the awe-inspiring presence of a member of the Great Race. He saw the fleshy body of Mickey "The Gun" Guinn.

From the corner of my eye, I glimpsed Hannah. She was half on the train, torn between leaving and staying to help me.

"Go," I said to her sternly. "Don't even think it. This host — I'm not worth it."

My words didn't budge her. She stood her ground, grasping the handrail along the inside of the train car entrance.

From some place distant, I heard a voice call "All aboard!"

I knew it wouldn't be long before someone would stumble upon this unfolding play; someone who wouldn't try to avoid the situation, but who would call the police. Even for a member of the Great Race time can be inconvenient.

There we stood, Dazzy and I, each watching the other, waiting for the first to make a move. Dazzy was tall, and stood erect in his finely pressed suit, with a revolver undoubtedly tucked away in a shoulder holster beneath his flashy clothing.

I, or rather Mickey, looked his usual dumpy self, with an ill-fitting suit, and as Dazzy undoubtedly assumed, weaponless. But Dazzy had overlooked the crumpled paper bag still in my hand. I held the top of the bag firmly with one hand, and felt the revolver inside with my other. Dazzy was so intent upon presenting an intimidating façade that he had yet to notice Mickey's *lunch.*

I settled my finger on the trigger. The bag rattled.

"Dazzy!" Hannah called. "Don't do it. It wasn't Mickey's idea. It was mine. I'll return the money."

Dazzy's smile broadened. He had a reptilian look about him. I couldn't help but wonder if he were descended from the race of intelligent reptiles that had once dominated the Earth several million years ago, another species humanity was oblivious to.

"Now you're talking kid," Dazzy said. "Forget all this and come back. Dutch will forget it all. He'll let bygones be bygones."

Right, I thought. That was as likely as humanity's survival.

Dutch Schultz was a human who had a life he didn't deserve. Except, unlike Hannah, his was far better than what he deserved. I admit, I have peeked into his future. As one might expect, his death is painful and protracted. It doesn't come until 1935, but when it does, he lingers for several days in the hospital, rambling incoherently. Actually, what he says does make sense to a member of the Great Race. He was inhabited prior to his death, and his memories were not properly eradicated. The irony was quite pleasant. Instead of comprehending the true nature of the Great Race, his limited mind was temporally confused, blending human myths of devils and angels to explain his *possession* by the Great Race. His dying words were so unsettling to humanity that there are those who struggled for decades to comprehend them.

For me, Hannah represented something of a problem. I understood her. She was an artist like me. But she couldn't pick her life, unlike me. This produced an emotion in me that was difficult to reconcile. While I loathed humanity, and longed for their inevitable demise so my species could dominate the world in the future, I pitied humans at the same time. The path I was about to take was forbidden to me. I was not permitted to *tinker* with the Great Plan. But I was an artist, and I had a need to satisfy my personal sense of aesthetics. Helping Hannah escape her present life and give her a new one, one without the likes of Dutch Schultz, seemed . . . pleasing. *Satisfying*. It appeased my higher sense of aesthetics.

"You can walk away from this, Mickey," Dazzy said. "Both of you can turn it around now. Just come back and talk to Dutch. He wants to work it out. Give him the fifty Gs and he'll forgive and forget."

Dazzy was beginning to repeat himself. I suspected he'd

reached the limit of his negotiating abilities.

Both my host and I truly disliked Dazzy. All his offer did was to rouse the suppressed persona of my host body, causing me to force it deeper into the unconscious portion of the host brain. Humans are such nosey beings. Even when they've been subjugated to an unconscious region of their own mind they still listen in on conversations. I am quite put off by the human unconscious and its bizarre abilities. I will be earnestly pleased to rid the world of these creatures. Even when you try to assist one, all they do is make it difficult.

"Lose yourself, Hannah," I said, determining to end this before the crowd started to return. "Dutch doesn't deal. You know that. He doesn't forgive. You know that too. Get on that train and don't come back. I'll keep Dutch occupied and buy you some time."

Something in my words must have finally broken through her stubborn nature. Quickly, and without a word, she vanished into the train. I could see that my words also had an affect upon Dazzy. I watched as his hand slid inside his pristine suit coat, searching for his gun.

I didn't wait to hear if he had another offer. He was a human. I despised him. My host despised him. Most everyone who encountered Dazzy despised him. So I applied pressure to the trigger of the revolver inside the bag.

Baam!

Not surprisingly, an astonished look formed on Dazzy's face. He was far from brilliant, and even further from smart.

Baam! Baam!

The second shot was to secure his death. The third was to satisfy my sense of aesthetics, and to quell the struggling persona of Mickey. He seemed content when Dazzy dropped to the ground with a heavy *thump*.

After shooting Dazzy, I didn't wait around. I dumped the paper bag in the nearest garbage can. I had no illusions that Dutch would come looking for me . . . Mickey. But that was my intention. Shortly after leaving Penn Station, after seeing Hannah's train roll away, I released the host body, allowing Mickey to return to full consciousness. I did not leave him with all of his memories. The recent memories relating to Hannah I exorcised from his mind. What I did leave was his encounter with Dazzy, and the knowledge that Dutch would come looking for him. By the time Mickey and Dutch sorted out their differences, mainly by Mickey's dying, I figured Hannah would be long forgotten.

I would have preferred to simply eradicate all memories of Hannah from Dutch; but long-term memories require the use of certain technologies that would attract attention to my indiscretions. This was personal art that had no influence upon the Great Plan, so there was no need to involve any other members of my species.

I do check on Hannah on occasion, whenever I'm in the area. She moved to a small town overflowing with greenery — it seems true artists have a passion for greenery. There she lived the remainder of her life, teaching young humans to sing. She did have a natural talent. She also had a life she deserved.

WIND DEMONS

—In 1886, the last free Apache surrendered to the United States

LIEUTENANT SETH DAVIS RAISED a hand, halting the patrol. The six men and horses behind clamored to a stop as the scout far in the lead trotted back to the group.

"What is it, Branton?" Davis asked the scout.

Sam Branton slouched in the saddle, his Remington-Hepburn resting across his lap. The man wore stained trousers, tucked into dusty boots, and a sweat-damp undershirt that was crisscrossed by red suspenders — a bit reminiscent of the Confederate Battle Flag. He jawed tobacco, forming a lump on one side of his mouth when he spoke.

"There were Apache down the canyon," Branton said.

Lieutenant Davis worked to steady his horse, doing his best to appear relaxed and in control. "*Are* or *were*?" he asked.

Branton shifted the lump from one cheek to the other, his small eyes black in the hot sun. He turned about, peering down the canyon.

"Well?" Davis said, lowering his voice.

"I reckon *were*," Branton said, and then turned to smile at the lieutenant. "Wouldn't you say?" When he spoke, his straggly mustache twitched like a rabbit's nose.

"You're the scout," Davis replied.

"That I am." His smile broadened, seemingly splitting Branton's visage. He returned his gaze to the canyon.

A narrow defile stretched before them, with jagged walls

flanking both sides. Thorn bush and rocks filled a bottom covered in reddish-brown dust; the afternoon sun cast short shadows here and there. The passage snaked back and forth until it vanished in a northerly direction. Lieutenant Davis knew every man on the patrol was thinking about the rumors, about the creatures that lived in the canyon.

"It's the buzzards," Branton said. "I think that makes it a *were*."

Davis gawked at the sky, spying several dark birds circling in the distance. He tugged at the brim of his hat to shade his eyes as best he could.

"Is that where Mr. Wheeler had his camp?" Davis said gruffly. "Or is that the location of some dead animal?"

"You get me every time you call him *Mister*," Branton replied, his words wallowing in a Southern drawl and tobacco. "Old Jacob Wheeler weren't never a Mister. Crazy as a bed bug, but not a Mister."

"Is that the site of his camp?" Davis said sternly.

"*Was*, I reckon," Branton said, still squinting at the sky. "The Apache is *were*, and Jacob is *was*, if you catch my drift."

Davis prodded his horse, and waved the patrol forward. Branton bounced alongside.

"Are you sure this is where . . . Wheeler staked his claim?" Davis asked. He could feel the scout's eyes upon him.

"Yep. 'Course, he never told nobody. It was never 'fficial. But when he came into town for supplies, I could see the dust on his clothes." Branton paused to spit, then continued. "I remembered the dust. Red. Couldn't be any other place than here. Being as it was his, and he clearly wanted to keep it private, I never ventured out. But when he didn't come in for supplies, a few folk got worried. They formed up and went looking for him–"

"Did you warn them about the Apaches?" Davis interrupted.

"No-sir, I didn't. I told 'em there was something much worse out here than that, and old Jacob was crazy for diggin' in this here canyon."

The patrol plodded through the valley, each soldier stealing glances at the ridge. In the distance, the vultures stopped their aerial dance and descended to dine on carrion.

"I'm amazed more attention wasn't given to your Indian ghost-stories," Davis said dryly. "I'm sure all manner of foul creature live in this canyon."

The Point had prepared Seth for war and command, but not for wild Apache, heat, and superstitious scouts. And this one, Davis decided, was just about old enough to have fought in the war. *What a damnable thing! A haggard Confederate scout leading a patrol of Union soldiers on a hunt for a missing miner.* He'd served with men he could trust at the reservation. But history books didn't record the deeds of a soldier who was nothing more than a bureaucrat. A field command — now that would prove his mettle. He'd already shown himself a competent officer when ushering savages onto the reservations. Now he would do the same in combat.

"You won't see 'em," Branton said.

"See what?"

"Apaches. If you see 'em, it's 'cause they want you to."

A narrow smile inched across Davis' face. "I see them all the time."

Branton spit again, almost as though it were a reply to Davis' arrogance. "Yes-sir. You fellows rounded 'em up and put 'em on the reservations, but not all of 'em. There are some still 'round here. And they protect this place." The dusty scout shook his head slowly. "They don't watch like they used to. That's how old Jacob made his claim. The Apaches you fellers didn't catch went south. That's where this bunch is from, down Texas way. But they came back too late. Least too late for old Jacob, I reckon."

"Or maybe they came back for him," Davis added smartly. "We'll round them all up. I can assure you of that."

✱ ✱ ✱

Soon the sun claimed a spot on the horizon, blazing red the lower it dropped. The approaching darkness caused Davis to coax a quicker pace from the men. He did not want to be ambushed in the canyon. The rocky bottom had gradual slopes, and the upper reaches climbed toward the sky in a nearly vertical fashion. Dotting the top of the ridges were scrub, and an occasional copse of pines, offering anyone above lovely cover.

If the patrol were caught below, it would be enfiladed — a tactical disaster.

"How much farther?" Davis asked, fatigue tinting his words.

"Not much longer," Branton said. He pointed to another twist. "Up there. Then we get to higher ground and Jacob's mine."

"Sergeant Morgan," Davis ordered. "Let's pick up the pace. I want to get there before sunset."

Directly behind the lieutenant rode Sergeant Timothy Morgan, the lead of the snaking column of cavalrymen. In response, Morgan repeated the order, and each rider quickened to a trot.

Sergeant Morgan had served in the Union cavalry for 20 years. Davis knew he was far too disciplined to question an order, but concern mingled in the sergeant's voice. *Doubt.* And the men could hear it as well. In the past, Davis had whipped the disobedient soldiers along with the defiant Apache. But he knew that type of discipline didn't work on patrols. He made a note to speak with Morgan when they returned to the fort. Maybe a show of his authority would train the soldiers properly.

With the sun ducking beneath the canyon walls, the group of men struggled up a path that ended at a camp. In the devilish red glow of the evening light, the remains of Jacob Wheeler were clearly visible. By now the vultures had left, and had taken most of his flesh.

Bile burned like whiskey in the back of Davis' throat. He placed a gloved hand over his mouth, hoping to conceal his reaction.

Branton dropped from his horse, leaving his rifle slung on the animal. With surprising agility, the scout scampered across the hard ground, halting before Jacob Wheeler.

The dead man hung from a makeshift pole, a rope pressing into the remaining bloated flesh of his throat. His clothes were shredded, innards spilled on the ground.

"Sergeant," Davis yelled. "Form a skirmish line around this area."

The men responded quickly, pulling carbines, scrambling to the large boulders around the camp. Each soldier clad in blue with yellow stripes on their trousers surveyed the terrain.

"Jake, you fool," Branton said as he stepped onto a rock and cut the man down. "You gone an done it now."

Lieutenant Davis hopped from his mount, and approached Sergeant Morgan. "Keep an eye out for Apache," Davis said softly. Davis trusted the Confederate scout less now than he did prior to entering the canyon. The lieutenant knew that many cowards had fled after the war, running West to avoid being punished for crimes. Many took up with Indians.

"Sir," the sergeant replied. "Sir, I do not believe this was Apache, or any other Indian I know of."

The moment had finally arrived — the moment Lieutenant Davis had been expecting. He learned of the difficulties of field commands at the Point. Soldiers do not question authority. Morgan would certainly be his first example when they completed this patrol.

"Sergeant," Davis said, locking Morgan's gaze. "You have a duty. I expect–"

A long, deep cry cut Davis' words short. The loathsome noise seemingly fell from the darkening vault above.

Immediately the remainder of the patrol twisted about, aiming carbines upward.

The men chattered among themselves, each trying to assign an animal to the wretched sound.

It repeated, but this time from a distance. Then quickly another mournful cry replied, this one nearby. The men hunkered down, swinging rifles this way and that.

"That ain't Apache work," Branton said from over Jacob Wheeler's body. "This —" he gestured at the mutilated corpse with the large knife in his hand — "this is some ceremonial offering, I reckon. But it was more than vultures that have been at him."

Quickly, Davis shot a look at Branton, then back to Morgan. Things were starting to slip. "Tend to the men, Sergeant. That is your duty. I make the decisions here."

Morgan snapped a quick salute, then dashed toward the men, revolver in hand.

Once again the fearsome cry echoed through the canyon. This time it started at a distance and seemed to glide right over the mining camp. Davis approached Branton.

"What game are you playing at?" Davis asked, hostile. As he spoke, he settled a hand on his Colt.

"What in tarn'ashun are you gibberin' 'bout?" Branton said. "You figure this is a hoax or somethin'? If so, then you're figurin' wrong." The scout shoved his knife into its leather sheaf. "There's something out there. And I'm guessin' it's a might hungry."

"Something?" Davis replied. "What do you take me for? Don't mistake me for some country fool. I know precisely what you're up to. You lured us out here, and now your savage friends are trying to spook my men."

Branton squinted, scratched the back of his head, and then spit. "I don't rightly know what you're tryin' to say. But I figure it's borderin' on something I won't like. So I'll not think on it now." He nodded toward the horseguard, struggling to keep the animals calm. "Those beasts ain't as blind as you, however. Something's got 'em spooked. And I think you'd be best off if you had a little of it too."

This time the cry came from a soldier. When Davis turned, a shadowy creature, twice the size of a horse, flapped leathery wings in the hot air, clawing at the screaming man. Carbines fired, muzzles flashed in the growing gloom. The report of the guns bounced off the canyon walls, fading as though fleeing.

The horses jumped and kicked, knocking down the horseguard. One by one the animals raced down the path into the defile. And there, beside his horse stood Branton. He tugged at the saddle bags, trying to steady the horse. Blankets, canteen and his rifle dropped to the ground as the horse broke free from the scout's hold.

Davis pulled his revolver and fired at the dark thing that clawed at the soldier.

Bullets buzzed and whistled. Finally the monster let loose a cry; the sound muffled the gunfire. The vile screech seeped into Davis' bones, sending tendrils of ice along his limbs. Then the creature vanished into the night.

Before the dust had settled, Sergeant Morgan was beside the downed soldier. Try as he might, Davis could not remember the wounded man's name.

"Post!" the lieutenant bellowed. With a brief hesitation, and a quick glance to Sergeant Morgan, the men hunkered down behind outcroppings and boulders, searching the murky sky for the flying nightmares.

Not entirely sure of what to do next, Davis kneeled alongside the dying soldier. Morgan uttered soothing words, lifting a canteen to the man's lips.

"Hold on, solider," Davis said weakly, chiding himself for not remembering the man's name. "We'll get you to a surgeon."

Morgan shot a glance at the lieutenant, his gaze cold.

"We can't stay out here," Branton interrupted, his arms cradling what he'd managed to pull from his horse. "Those critters ain't goin' to just up and leave."

Davis stood, shoulders square, back straight, the definitive image of an officer. Methodically he removed his tan riding gloves, tugging one finger free at a time, intentionally remaining silent all the while.

"Lord-oh-mighty! You are as thick as mud in the Spring," Branton exclaimed. He turned from the lieutenant and plodded toward the cave opening that Jacob had used as a mine entrance.

"You might think Indian tales are hokum," the scout said over his shoulder. "But when you lose enough men, you'll come 'round. I've seen your kind before. Back at Antietam and Fredericksburg. Too dull witted to organize a kitchen detail, and too damned stubborn to stop a disastrous attack."

Branton's fiery words ignited the other men's imaginations. They shared glances with one another, concern and doubt washing across their countenances.

Lieutenant Seth Davis trailed after the scout, stopping outside the mine's entrance. He leveled the Colt revolver at the man's back. The hammer *clicked* under his thumb. But his finger was stayed by the cool touch of a blade at his throat.

"Gray Wolf is a brother," said the Apache standing beside Davis.

The remainder of the patrol spun, aiming at the Indian. A few curses escaped mouths, amazed at the Apache's stealth.

"Hold!" Sergeant Morgan ordered, although the command lacked enthusiasm.

Somewhere in the dark distance echoed another terrible screech.

"I knew you were in league with these savages, Branton," said Davis through clenched teeth. "Damnable Rebel coward."

Barely visible in the fading sanguine glow of the setting sun, Branton crouched, emptying his arms on the cavern floor.

"Don't," Branton said to the Indian. "He's foolish."

"I know this," the Apache said. "I know who he is. I've seen him herd my people like cattle onto reservations."

"Sergeant," Davis said. "If this savage does not lower his weapon, shoot him."

"Hold on a minute," Branton hollered. "This Apache is not a threat to us." The scout signaled for the Indian to lower the hunting knife.

Slowly, the Apache pulled the blade away, and snugged it into a sheath.

Standing next to Davis, the Apache seemed nearly a foot shorter. His long black hair hid much of is broad face; a worn buckskin shirt and pants covered a lean body.

Without a word, the soldiers surrounded the intruder. Davis now focused his revolver on the Indian, but occasionally stole glances at the sky.

"Bring him inside," Davis said. "I think we've already sprung Branton's trap."

Sergeant Morgan commandeered a soldier and carried the wounded cavalryman into the stony shelter, while the others directed the Apache and Branton.

Once inside, Davis had the scout and the Apache tied and set against one of the rugged walls. From the maw of the cave, the red glow of the sun faded into blackness.

While the men busily set fires and made torches, Davis questioned his captives. "What are those things outside? And what were your intentions? Revenge, I suspect. Revenge for losing the wars."

A coarse laugh escaped Branton. "You are a fool. A damned fool, Davis. You can't see what's goin' on before your very eyes."

"And what is that? Two cowards who've used some Indian trick to murder an innocent man and tried to kill more." As he spoke, he waved toward the members of the patrol.

"Those are air spirits outside," the Apache said. "Demons of the wind. Long ago, before the mountains and before the moon, my fathers' fathers trapped the wind spirits in the earth. Once they hunted Apache, Navaho, Lakota, Comanche, and others, feeding upon the evil inside them. Inside men. But the shaman trapped them beneath the ground, and their anger made the mountains. Now they've been set free."

"Sergeant Morgan," Davis said. "Set a guard at that entrance." The lieutenant then straightened his hat, and started pacing the length of the cave. "You want me to believe that Jacob Wheeler unburied these things — and then they strung him up and ate him?"

"No," the Apache said. "The demons killed him. I tied him to a sacred pole–"

"Hanged him!" Davis yelled.

"Yes. It is the way an offering is made. But it didn't work. He had already been killed by them."

"So you set him out there to be skinned by the vultures."

"It is the way of the world."

"The savage world, maybe," Davis spat. "But not the civilized world. We don't believe in air spirits and such nonsense."

"It wasn't the miner. It is the *indaa* — the white man. He has brought great evil to this land. The demons can smell the pain of the Apache on reservations, of the foul deeds of soldiers. It is you who summoned them. This cave was simply how they arrived."

"I refuse to believe that. This is nothing more than some wild animal that the Apaches have had trapped in a hole." Davis twisted toward the Indian, grabbing him by his shirt. "If I put you out there, they would attack you just the same as they would a white man."

"They would," the Indian said softly. "I have evil in me. But I would not quench them. They would stay, longing for more."

Davis shoved the captive against the hard wall. "Ha!"

Above the heated words, the inhuman calls of the flying demons filled the confined space, growing in volume and agitation.

"Sir," Sergeant Morgan interrupted. "I don't figure they'll stay outside much longer. Maybe we should barricade the opening."

The lieutenant took a moment from his tirade to consider

the situation. "That opening is too wide. It is indefensible. Gather what material you can. We'll construct a defensive position here."

"You might want to start believin' in *this* Indian tale," Branton said smugly. "The way I figure it, those rifles ain't goin' to stop them demons from getting' in here. Neither is a hastyworks."

"Then maybe we should hang you outside," Davis said bitterly. "You'd certainly satisfy them."

"No," said the Apache. "Gray Wolf is a good man. It is the evil of other men, and the weakness of the Apache that keep the dark ones here. They can be satisfied for now, but they will return."

Davis considered the words for a few moments. Decisions had been easier at the Fort Apache reservation, when he'd been dealing with re-settlement. An Indian like this one he would have simply killed, making the rest fall into line. But the situation was different out here, away from loyal men who'd stand to protect him. Still, this was a part of a field command. Decisions needed to be made quickly. He knew the price of battle was lives. His duty was to persevere and limit casualties. Hard choices required strong leaders.

"Sergeant Morgan, I fear that . . ." he paused, turning toward the dying soldier.

"Private Hobbs, Sir."

"Yes, Private Hobbs. He is in a bad way. He did his duty, but he can still serve."

Morgan's eyes widened. "He's alive, Sir. You can't be suggesting that—"

"You're correct, Sergeant. I'm not *suggesting*. I'm giving you an order. Take his body outside and tie him to the post. He's still a soldier, and he can serve in the capacity best suited to the needs of the United States."

The other men under Davis' command stopped working on the fires and the works. The guard at the opening even turned at the sound of the lieutenant's thundering voice. As though to punctuate Davis' proclamation, a long, mournful cry danced through the canyon.

Stunned, Morgan, Timothy Morgan from Ohio, stood before

his commander, eyes narrowed, mouth drawn tight.

Insubordination was the greatest threat in dire circumstances. To cut off the head of that snake, Davis drew his revolver.

"That is an order, Sergeant."

"If you intend to shoot me, Lieutenant, then you best get it over with. Because I will not follow that order."

Davis cocked the revolver.

The sound of two carbines *snicking* followed.

Slowly, Davis surveyed the mine. In the flickering firelight, the two privates who'd been crafting torches now held rifles. Each aimed at Davis.

Shadows danced on the walls, reproducing a carnival-like scene, distorting the shapes of the men. Davis' cast the largest shadow, but through some trick of the flames, it was the most malformed.

"This is mutiny," Davis declared.

"It *was* 'bout to be murder," Branton said. "Now it seems like it *is* going to be justice, if you catch my drift."

"This man has a black heart," the Indian said. "His evil will satisfy the demons. They wait for him."

"I will not tolerate this!" Davis yelled. "Everyone of you will be brought up on charges! Do you understand me?"

"Yes-sir," Morgan said. "Now surrender your revolver."

Astonishment twisted Davis' face into an ugly shape. The thought of shooting the sergeant flicked through his mind. But it served little purpose. Instead, he relied upon the power of his authority as an officer, and the fear of punishment to allow him to control the situation. Gingerly, he handed his Colt to Morgan.

"You don't understand the circumstances," Lieutenant Davis said. "If you do this Sergeant, you'll be in command. You'll have to make difficult decisions, ones that you are not trained to make."

Morgan nodded. "I guess so. But fighting in two wars has toughened me up a touch."

"What you're doing serves no purpose," Davis said.

"Lieutenant, you are still a soldier, and you can serve in the capacity best suited to the needs of the United States."

"You heard the Indian," Davis said, his words more heated

than frightened. "Sacrificing someone won't stop them. It'll only pacify them. My plan was to stand ground until reinforcements arrived in the morning. With greater numbers we can kill them."

"The demons will take the offering," the Indian said, but it won't banish them. The spirit of my people must awaken, and the spirit of the white man. They must remember their past before the demons will return to the earth."

"But it will stop them for a while, won't it?" one of the privates offered.

"Yes. For a while," the Apache replied.

"You can't trust a savage," Davis blurted. "He's talking about demons."

"I can vouch for him," Branton said. "In '65 I came out here. It was Geronimo here who taught me the ways of the Apache. I admit, he fled the reservation in '75, but I'd done the same thing." The scout turned to Davis. "I've seen what you do to his people. I wouldn't tolerate it either."

"I am Apache; I am Geronimo. But I had forgotten what it meant to be Apache. Someday, I hope to awaken the spirit in all my people. We will remember, and these demons will return to the earth."

"Good enough for me," one private said. The others nodded.

The report of a carbine roared through the rocky chamber. The guard at the opening fired at one of the winged demons trying to enter. One-two-three shots came from his repeating rifle. The other soldiers clambered forward, joining in the fray. The withering fusillade eventually forced the creature away.

Morgan kept the Colt pointed at the lieutenant.

"Morgan . . ." Davis said.

"Time is running short," the sergeant said. "I don't like this. But I've been told by many-a-officer that the sacrifices of the few serve the greater numbers." Morgan motioned for the lieutenant to move forward.

"You go to battle now," Geronimo said to Davis. "I'll join you some day."

Lieutenant Seth Davis' face soured at the words. "I"ll never fight alongside a savage." Then he squared his shoulders, and marched forward. "This will do little good, except place my name in the history books. I'll be remembered as a hero, and the rest of you will be forgotten. Erased from the world. What I do now is for posterity. I will be avenged."

The sergeant followed on the lieutenant's heels. They emerged into the blackness, with only the light of a torch carried by another soldier to guide them. Without complaint, Davis stepped upon the rock, and hooked the rope around his neck.

"I'll see you in Hell," Davis said.

Morgan nodded. "You will at that."

After the two soldiers re-entered the cave, the scream came. It belonged to Davis. He howled and cried, his voice mixing with the chilling screeches of the demons. Then the stillness of night returned.

When the men emerged the next morning, they found the mutilated body of Jacob Wheeler, but no indication of Lieutenant Seth Davis. Not even his uniform remained. Without another word, the patrol started back on foot with Branton leading the way. The Apache strode into the countryside alone.

ABOUT THE AUTHOR

WILLIAM JONES writes in various genres, including mystery, horror, science fiction, dark fiction, historical and young adult. He has edited several fiction anthologies and magazines. Occasionally he dabbles in the role-playing industry, where he has published articles and gaming supplements for a variety of publishers.

Presently William is the editor of *Dark Wisdom* magazine. When not writing or editing, he teaches English at a university in Michigan.

Visit his website at: www.williamjoneswriter.com